DESPERATE
MEASURES

DESPERATE MEASURES

LAURA SUMMERS

G. P. PUTNAM'S SONS • AN IMPRINT OF PENGUIN GROUP (USA) INC.

G. P. PUTNAM'S SONS
A division of Penguin Young Readers Group.
Published by The Penguin Group.
Penguin Group (USA) Inc., 375 Hudson Street, New York, NY 10014, U.S.A.
Penguin Group (Canada), 90 Eglinton Avenue East, Suite 700, Toronto, Ontario M4P 2Y3, Canada
(a division of Pearson Penguin Canada Inc.).
Penguin Books Ltd, 80 Strand, London WC2R 0RL, England.
Penguin Ireland, 25 St. Stephen's Green, Dublin 2, Ireland
(a division of Penguin Books Ltd.).
Penguin Group (Australia), 250 Camberwell Road, Camberwell, Victoria 3124, Australia
(a division of Pearson Australia Group Pty Ltd).
Penguin Books India Pvt Ltd, 11 Community Center, Panchsheel Park, New Delhi—110 017, India.
Penguin Group (NZ), 67 Apollo Drive, Rosedale, North Shore 0632, New Zealand
(a division of Pearson New Zealand Ltd).
Penguin Books (South Africa) (Pty) Ltd, 24 Sturdee Avenue, Rosebank, Johannesburg 2196, South Africa.
Penguin Books Ltd, Registered Offices: 80 Strand, London WC2R 0RL, England.

First American edition published in 2011 by G. P. Putnam's Sons,
a division of Penguin Young Readers Group, 345 Hudson Street, New York, NY 10014.
G. P. Putnam's Sons, Reg. U.S. Pat. & Tm. Off.
Also published in Great Britain by Piccadilly Press in 2010.
Published simultaneously in Canada. Printed in the United States of America. Text set in Paradigm.

Library of Congress Cataloging-in-Publication Data
Summers, Laura, 1960– Desperate measures / Laura Summers.   p. cm.
Summary: Thirteen-year-old Vicky, her brain-damaged twin sister, and her delinquent little brother
run away together to keep from being split up by the foster care system.
[1. Brothers and sisters—Fiction. 2. Twins—Fiction. 3. People with mental disabilities—Fiction.
4. Foster home care—Fiction. 5. Runaways—Fiction. 6. Home—Fiction.] I. Title.
PZ7.S95454De 2011 [Fic]—dc22 2010023210
ISBN 978-0-399-25616-5

1 3 5 7 9 10 8 6 4 2

To my family
With thanks to Lucy, Gaia, Anne and Sara

CHAPTER 1

Rhianna

My name is Rhianna Jane Davies but my twin sister Vicky always calls me Rhi. I'm much taller than her, but because she's forty-seven and a half minutes older than me, she's always trying to boss me around. When she tells me I've spilled my yogurt or put my T-shirt on backward or something, I pretend I can't hear her and start singing really loud. Then I call her a sticky slob bottom and that really gets on her nuckets. She makes that face—the one where her mouth stretches out sideways. She looks like she's going to explode, but she hasn't so far. Most times she just yells at me and stomps off, banging the door so loud it makes my ears hurt.

It's our birthday tomorrow. We're going to be

thirteen, and I can't wait. I made Vicky a card—it's got sparkly stuff stuck on it and some tinsel I found in the closet under the stairs. Jamie helped me spell the words and wipe off all the glue so Vicky can open it. Jamie's our little brother. He's got black caterpillar eyebrows and hair that sticks up like a toilet brush. He's ten and always getting into trouble.

I'm not in the same class as Vicky because I'm in the Special Unit. It's not very special, except the ceiling's got a big brown stain because the roof leaks when it rains. Vicky gets really angry if the other kids say nasty things to me. Once when Charlene Slackton called me Der-Brain, Vicky went up to her and said she'd like to see her survive for nearly an hour without enough air to breathe. That's what happened when I was born, you see. I was coming out of my mom's you-know-what and I got stuck. Probably because I've got really big feet. Size eights. Vicky only takes fives, and Jamie's a teensy four and a half.

CHAPTER 2

Vicky

*I*t must have been five o'clock in the morning when Rhianna woke up me up. Five A.M. and she's all excited and yelling in my ear.

"Vicky, come on, Vicky, let's go down and see what presents we've got!"

I ignored her for as long as I could, but when she ripped my quilt off and started bouncing up and down on my bed, all 125 pounds of her, that was it. I'd had enough. She drives me bonkers. It's really weird—although she's got this amazing memory for things that happened years ago, she's got absolutely no idea about time—we're talking "big hand" and "little hand" here, and even then she still hasn't got a clue. Most days she doesn't even know what day of the week it is or whether she's just eaten her breakfast, lunch or dinner.

"Get off, Rhi! Go back to sleep!" I yelled.

But she wouldn't. She disappeared off downstairs to wait for Mr. Mailman. After twenty minutes there was no sound, so I went down to check she hadn't electrocuted herself or flooded the kitchen, or both. She was sitting on the doormat.

"Come on, Rhi. Back to bed. . . ."

"But Dad might have sent us something."

"The mailman won't be here for another two hours and even then he . . ."

I stopped and looked at her, sitting awkwardly on the mat, her legs crossed like a badly jointed puppet's and her wide gray eyes fixed expectantly on the mail slot. I didn't like to burst her bubble, but things were different now. We were on our own. Without Mom and Dad, I mean. Mom died just over two years ago, and Dad . . . well . . . I don't want to go into that right now, but he's not around anymore. It's not all bad news, though. We've been fostered by a lovely couple named Paul and Sarah for the last eight months. It's meant we've had to go to new schools, but at least we're finished with all those lousy children's homes. Now, they really were the pits.

I could see Rhianna wasn't going to budge. In the end

I gave up, pulled the throw off the couch and tucked it around her because her hands and feet were going bluey-purple. I went into the kitchen and made a cup of tea, wondering whether Matt had got me a birthday card.

Matt is this gorgeous boy in my class. Don't get me wrong, he isn't actually my boyfriend or anything . . . but he was meeting me at the end of the road, and we were walking up to school together. My friend Rosie said I should consider myself as having engaged his attentions. (It's okay—she's a bit weird, she talks like that.) Anyway, you should have seen the look on Charlene Slackton's face when she heard about it; she was sooooo jealous because he's rated the hottest boy in our grade. And he likes me. Me! Vicky "Shrimp-Face" Davies.

Maybe I should explain. I'm really short and wear flat, sensible shoes for school (thanks to Sarah). I have curly strawberry blond hair that never does what I want it to (think ginger fuzz ball), I blush when I'm embarrassed (too much of the time) and have tons of freckles (say no more). Since I've been at this new school, I've made just one friend—Rosie—who's the school brain and reads Jane Austen novels instead of teen mags. Charlene has long blond hair down to her waist, wears really trendy clothes and high-heeled shoes that she can hardly walk in, and everyone who's anyone would chop their right arm off and beat themselves with the soggy end if it meant they could be in her gang. Except Rosie, of course, who wouldn't see the point, and me . . . maybe. Anyway, I blew my chances of ever being one of Charlene's best buddies when she teased Rhi and I told her exactly where to go.

When the mailman finally came, there was a letter for Sarah and a few cards for us. Rhi was opening all our cards as Paul and Sarah came downstairs.

"Aren't you going to sing us both 'Happy Birthday'?" I joked.

Sarah smiled and was about to say something but suddenly grimaced, sucked in her breath and rubbed her hand across her stomach. "Oooowww."

"You all right, love?" Paul asked. Sarah nodded and forced a smaller, tighter smile.

"I'm fine. But I think we're going to have a karate champ on our hands!"

Paul and Sarah have been the best thing to happen to us in a long while, and now things are set to get even better. Although she's pretty ancient (she must be at least forty-three), Sarah's going to have a baby! They were over the moon when they found out—and so were we when they told us we weren't going to be moved on again. Hooray! They'd decided they would carry on fostering us, baby and all. Jamie and I want it to be a boy; Rhianna's holding out for a girl, but Paul and Sarah say they don't care as long as it's healthy. So in a few months' time, we'll all be up to our armpits in diapers, bootees and baby vomit, and believe it or not, we're all looking forward to it.

Rhianna was busy sorting through the cards. She desperately wanted one with a 13 pin attached to it. There was a card for each of us from Mrs. Frankish. She's our social worker, but Jamie's managed to convince Rhi that she's really a witch because she's got a mole on her face with hairs growing out of it. She'd spelt Rhianna's name wrong, as usual, but had boosted our card count by 50 percent. There was nothing from Dad. When Rhi realized, her big gray eyes started to water and her face crumpled.

"Never mind, Rhi," I said, hugging her as she towered over me. "Maybe there aren't any mailboxes where he is."

Paul looked up from buttering some toast, and I felt my face reddening. "Dad's doing a really important job delivering medicine and food to all those refugees," I whispered to her when he was out of earshot. There was no way I wanted Rhianna or Jamie understanding where Dad really was. I didn't want anyone to know. It was a big black secret, and it was better if it stayed that way. When we first arrived at Paul and Sarah's, I sneaked a look at our paperwork while Mrs. Frankish was busy chatting. I scanned the pages detailing all the children's homes we'd

been in and then saw the large, hastily scribbled words—
No contact with dad. I remember feeling a huge wave of
relief as I realized that was it; no further explanation was
needed: Mrs. Frankish had rubbed him out of our lives.

Rhi gave me her card, and I made a massive fuss over
it. I knew she'd been making it for about two weeks, but I
pretended it was a big surprise. It was like the sort of thing
Jamie used to bring home from preschool, all smudged
with paint and big, wonky letters. I gave her another big
hug and told her it was my best card. She looked so proud,
I knew she believed me. Then I gave her a present, a
Furby—she's wanted one for ages—and, thinking maybe
this was a good time, I broke the news that she'd have to
walk to school with Jamie. I didn't want to look after her,
today of all days. She'd spoil everything. She always did.

Whoa! Big mistake. You'd have thought I'd told her
she had to stick her head in a bucket of worms, she made
such a fuss. Talk about an instant thunderstorm.

"I hate you!" she yelled. "I was going to give you one
of my Barbies for your present"—she'd cut the hair off
them both playing hairdressers last week—"but I'm not
now. You . . . you . . . conkhog!"

Don't ask me what a conkhog is, I haven't a clue. It's
just one of Rhianna's special words she reserves for when
she's losing it. She snatched back her card and sat on it.

Paul tried to calm her down, but I know what she's like when she gets worked up. It's better to leave her alone, or it just gets worse. Anyway, I thought, I'll make it up to her tonight. Sarah had let me buy her a cake—it cost a ton and looked totally lame with bright blue icing, but it had a picture of her favorite boy band on it. So I went out into the hall, got my school backpack and slipped quietly out the front door.

CHAPTER 3

Rhianna

All boys are vom. And boys called Matt are the vommiest of all. She could have let me come. I wouldn't have said anything. I could have walked behind them—they wouldn't have known I was there. I can walk really quietly, even when I've got my clodhoppers on.

I hate walking to school with Jamie. Something always happens. This time he said we had to go past one of the houses really quickly in case some boy saw us, and he did, so Jamie shouted, "Leg it!" and we had to run. He nearly made me fall over because we were going so fast. I got a stitch, but Jamie still wouldn't stop. We ran up to Sam's house (that's Jamie's friend) and banged on the door. Sam's mom answered, and the boy ran off shouting that he and his friends were going to beat Jamie up after school. Jamie yelled back that he didn't care, but his face went all chalky like it did when Mrs. Frankish told us that we weren't allowed to live with Dad anymore.

We went back the way we came and up to the woods. Jamie and Sam showed me their camp. It's a secret, though, so don't tell anyone. Only Jamie, Sam and me knew about it. They'd made a little den out of branches and ferns. It was lovely inside, all green and fuzzy.

We spent ages messing around. Jamie and Sam were making the den bigger, and I made some delicious stew. It's ever so easy. You just get a load of leaves and mud and stuff, put them in a hole in the ground and mix it all up with a long stick. I didn't have any water, so I used my break-time drink. I had to pick out a couple of bugs, but it looked all right.

"Let's come here again tomorrow before school," said Jamie.

"Yeah. I'll knock for you both really early," Sam told us.

When Jamie dropped me off at the school gates, everyone had already gone in. Mrs. Edwards was standing outside, talking to Vicky.

"Where have you been, Rhianna Davies?" Vicky shouted. Her eyes were all red and puffy. I looked down and kept quiet. I wasn't going to tell her about Jamie's camp.

Mrs. Edwards said there was no harm done and Vicky had better get to her class. My class did cooking all morning, and I made cheese straws. Except you couldn't blow through them. They just go soggy.

I saved Vicky my three biggest cheese straws. I wrapped them up in some foil Mrs. Edwards gave me, but when I saw Vicky after school she said she didn't want any. She said she was still mad at me about this morning.

We were walking down the hall when suddenly she stopped and turned around and started staring at the bulletin board.

"What's the matter, Vick?" I asked, but she didn't say anything. Then this tall boy came up to her and she went all red. Even her neck. She looked like a big red tomato.

"You look like a big red tomato, Vicky," I said. She didn't answer, so I said it again but much louder this time. "Vicky. I said you look like a big red tomato."

"Shut . . . up," she said with her teeth gritty, then she grinned at the tall boy all smiley-toothy.

It was Vomitty Matt. He saw my cheese straws wrapped up in the foil and said, "What's that?" I said cheese straws, and he said could he have one. I didn't want to give him one, but then I thought if he was my friend too, Vicky would let me walk to school with them tomorrow. He took two. He was only supposed to take one. Do you know, some people can't even count.

"You must be Vicky's cousin," he said with a grin.

"We're sisters," I said. "Twins."

Vicky was looking at her shoes.

"Oh," he said. "Vicky told me you were cousins . . ."

I heard her call after me, but I didn't stop. I ran past the bathrooms. Charlene Slackton was outside, leaning on the wall, talking to another girl. They laughed and Charlene stuck out her foot and the other girl said "loser" as I tripped.

I was scared, so I got up right away and ran out of the entrance, through the gates and up the road. Vicky was shouting at me to stop, but I didn't. I ran across the road. A car slammed on its brakes, and the driver opened his window and shouted rude words at me.

Vicky caught me and pulled me back onto the sidewalk. She was really angry. "You stupid idiot! You could have been run over!"

I pulled away from her. "Leave me alone."

"You know you're not allowed to go home on your own. You know that!"

"I hate you, Vicky."

"Good."

"I wish I didn't have a sister. Especially a horrible twin sister."

"The feeling's mutual."

"You're mutual too. . . . And smelly. Really, really smelly!" I shouted at her.

We turned around and started walking home. I didn't want her walking next to me, so every time she caught up, I raced ahead. It really got on her nuckets. Serve her right. I wished she *was* my cousin. Then I wouldn't have to see her every day or share a room with her and have to listen to her snoring like a hippo every night.

When we got home, Mrs. Frankish was there. I asked her if she'd got me a present, but she just sort of mumbled something. Paul came in looking all serious. Mrs. Frankish said she had something very important to talk to us about. I told her I knew all about having babies already because of Sarah, and it's really gross. Paul sat down and told us that Sarah was in the hospital. I asked if she was having her baby now, but Mrs. Frankish said it was much too early. "So what's she doing, then?" I said. Mrs. Frankish said Sarah wasn't well and she was going to have to stay in the hospital so they could keep a really close eye on her and the baby to make sure everything went okay. Paul kept shuffling about and saying he was sorry and then he told us he wouldn't be able to look after us for a while. I said was Sarah going to go away like Mom, and he just started crying, so I gave him my last cheese straw. He didn't eat it. He just kept looking at it and rolling it on the table like it was a twig or something.

Jamie burst in. He was all out of breath and he had blood on his face. He wiped it off with his sleeve, but no one noticed except me because they were all crying except Mrs. Frankish, who was patting Paul's hand. Some of her nail varnish was chipped off, so I had a good look, but I didn't see any black. (Witches have black fingernails, Jamie told me.) Jamie said, "What's up?" and she explained it all over again. When he asked who we were going to stay with, Paul just looked at Mrs. Frankish and didn't say anything.

Jamie said no way was he going back to those rude word, rude word, very rude word children's homes. Mrs. Frankish didn't even tell him off for swearing—she just sighed and said we couldn't go back there anyway because they were all full up. I asked, "Where we going, then?" and there was another big silence. Then Mrs. Frankish said that there was a lovely school that I could go to, and they had a swimming pool, and you didn't go home when lessons were over—you stayed and had a sleepover every night. I always wanted to have a sleepover, but my friend Maxine can never come to stay because she has funny fits when she goes to sleep. I said great, I can't wait, but then Vicky said no way was I going to be packed off like that.

"But you'll come too, Vick," I said, "and Jamie. I'll tell them you don't like swimming."

I've got my five-hundred-meter badge. Vicky says she can swim, but she can't—I've seen her—and she puts her foot down all the time.

Mrs. Frankish said they couldn't come because it wasn't suitable for them. I asked why not, and she said it was a special school. I told her Vicky and Jamie were special, and she just nodded and said of course they were. But then she said she had managed to find two families who could each foster one child for a while. Mrs. Frankish said she was sorry, but it was all arranged. We were going tomorrow.

CHAPTER 4
Vicky

I followed her out of the room.

"Tomorrow? Tomorrow! No way!" I yelled. "You can't do this to us!"

"I've been running around half the afternoon trying to find places for you all," Mrs. Frankish said with a sigh. "Believe me, we're lucky to have got what we have."

"We? WE! It's not we, it's nothing to do with 'we'! *You're* not going to be shoved away with some horrible family or carted off to some dumb school where you don't know anyone and no one knows you."

She turned and looked at me. "There's no point in making a fuss, Vicky," she said, with that "I'm a caring and concerned social worker" look on her face. "There *is* no other option."

I could feel the anger boiling up in me. She must have realized, because then she said, "I'll just leave you to have a little time out on your own to calm down a bit, then you'd better start getting your stuff together." She started to walk out but stopped at the doorway.

"Oh," she said casually, like this sort of thing happened all the time, "I've got some trash bags if you haven't got enough suitcases."

Trash bags! That just about summed it up. She was shuffling us around as if we were no more than a few bags of trash to be tidied out of her way.

Well, what about what *we* wanted? Didn't that matter? That stupid woman had so much power over us. It was criminal. And what was worse, she pretended that everything she did was in our best interest or some other garbage. She didn't really give a hoot.

I didn't want to live miles away with people I didn't know, I didn't want to leave my school, and I didn't want to leave Rosie and Matt. It wasn't fair. I'm not going, I thought. And I'm not leaving Rhianna and Jamie either. Jamie was always in trouble; if he was shoved somewhere else he'd really go off the rails, and Rhianna was such a baby it would be cruel. She might be a royal pain in the butt 99 percent of the time, but she was my sister and she needed me.

But what could I do? I grabbed my cell and dialed Rosie's number. I hadn't known her for long, and she was pretty odd sometimes, but she was my friend and, boy, was I a friend in need. Maybe she could help; after all she was supposed to have an IQ of three billion or something. The second I heard her voice, I realized I was living in cloud cuckoo land. How could I have been so stupid? How could I have possibly said, "Hey, Rosie, will your parents put me up for a bit? Oh, and there's my delinquent little brother and my brain-damaged twin sister too. . . ." So I twittered on about Matt, and she promised to lend me a book of seventeenth-century romantic poetry. I didn't get around to telling her that tomorrow I'd be living somewhere else, without Jamie, without Rhianna, and I probably wouldn't see her or Matt again for ages. I don't know how I did it, really. Old Mackintosh, my drama teacher, should have put me up for the lead role in the school play. Except I won't be at the same school, I thought. I'll be at yet another new place with no friends because I can't get into anyone's stupid little clique, and I'll be spending every break time head down, walking purposefully around pretending I'm just on my way to meet up with my fantastic gang of supercool friends.

Hopeless. It was all totally hopeless.

CHAPTER 5

Rhianna

Mrs. Frankish made us dinner because the hospital called Paul and he had to leave. He looked really scared, and when I asked, he told me he had to take Sarah a fresh nightie. She'd only been there one day! It must be a really fancy hospital, and if you spill your dinner or something, you have to change your nightie or they shout at you and tell you off. When Mom was in the hospital, they never told her off, and she used to knock things over all the time.

There was this lady there and she used to come and do Mom's lovely long hair every week until it went all thin and wispy and then she'd only let me do it. I'd bring in all my barrettes and scrunchies and lay them on the bedcover,

20

and she'd pick which ones she wanted. Then I'd put them in really gently and bring the little mirror over and show her, and it would make her smile for a little while.

I didn't have time to finish my card for Sarah. It said GET WE. After Paul rushed off, I went into the kitchen and told Mrs. Frankish he had forgotten to take the clean nightie with him and Sarah would get into big trouble. She said couldn't I see she was busy cooking and told me to go away and stop fussing. She had three blobs of red sploppy stuff on her black jacket. They looked like ladybugs.

Dinner was yucky. It was supposed to be spaghetti hoops with little sausages, but because she's a witch, I think she put in some chopped worms or frogs' eyeballs when no one was looking. Jamie ate mine. Vicky said she was a vegetibblarian and made herself a ham sandwich when Mrs. Frankish was on the phone. Then I had a big surprise. Vicky got out a birthday cake! It was so beautiful! We put candles on it, and Vicky lit them and then I blew them all out twice and made two wishes, but I can't tell you what I wished for because if I do, they won't come true. Sorry. I had three and a half pieces of cake because Vicky left most of hers.

After dinner we went out into the backyard to Jamie's tree house. He didn't usually let us in, but he said we could to get away from Mrs. Frankish.

I loved Jamie's tree house. It was like a little wooden nest, but instead of soft feathers to line it, he'd pinned up all the postcards from Dad. He's a truck driver and when he used to drive somewhere, he would always send Jamie a card. He's got millions and billions and trillions. I tried to count them once, but I kept getting it wrong. It's a good thing Dad doesn't send them anymore because there isn't any space left.

Once at school Jamie told this boy Ollie Stanmore about them all, but Ollie didn't believe him, so Jamie whacked him. Jamie does a lot of whacking. I heard Mrs. Frankish tell Sarah that it's because he's got a lot of emotional baggage, but that's not true—he's only got his school backpack. Sarah and Paul had to go and see Mr. Biggs and Mrs. Featherstone because Jamie gave Ollie a nosebleed once and he nearly got exbooted from school. Jamie said he didn't care and it served him right, but Ollie told me that Mrs. Featherstone asked what would your dad say if he knew what you'd done, and Jamie started crying. He never cries. Once he fell off the jungle gym in the park and broke his arm, but he didn't even cry then and the bone was all poking out and there was blood everywhere.

I tried to count all the postcards again. I got to twenty-seven but then I gave up because I couldn't concentrate. I wished we still lived with Dad. Every Friday night when he came back from work, he used to bring me a big roll of Smarties. He'd watch me line them up on the table in their different colors and then I'd count them and do some sums before I ate them. He always helped me get the answers right. Sometimes, when he used to come home late, Mom would let us wait up for him. He'd come through the front door and we'd run up to him in a crazy pack. He was the strongest man in the whole world. He could pick us all up at once and swing us around, and Mom would laugh and yell at him to be careful. Sometimes when I try to talk to Vicky about Mom and Dad, she says there's no point remembering anything because it's like watching someone else's home movie. I don't know what she means, and she gets all mad if I ask.

Vicky was in a real mood in the tree house. Vomitty Matt was coming around later, and Mrs. Frankish had said she couldn't go out. She had to pack all her stuff. We were all sitting on the moldy cushions when Jamie told us his Big Idea. He said we should run away because then they couldn't split us up. I looked over at Vicky. She was biting her nails like they were really itching her or something.

I said, "Can we run away to Disneyland?"

"We'll go somewhere better," said Jamie.

I looked at Vicky again. "What about it?"

"What about what?" She sounded really snappy.

"Running away."

"They're only going to split us up for a while—when the baby's born, they'll have us back."

Vicky got up, but Jamie tugged at her arm. "What if they don't?" he said.

"They've promised."

"But what if something happens or they change their minds?"

Vicky made a face, then stared out of the little tree house doorway. "It's a stupid idea; we've got nowhere to go."

"We could go to my secret camp in the woods," said Jamie, picking up one of the postcards from the floor. "Just for a bit. Until everything's all right again. It would be like when we went on vacation with Mom and Dad to Great-Auntie Irene's."

The last time we went to Great-Auntie Irene's, we all camped out in a tent on a little island in the middle of this big lake.

Great-Auntie Irene's dog, Jip, came with us and we all got in the rowing boat and rowed out to the island. We made a campfire and cooked potatoes in foil and marshmallows on sticks. The potatoes were all black on the outside and hard on the inside. Mom wasn't going to let us eat them—she said we'd be sick. But we did and we weren't. She was the one that kept being sick. She never even ate any potato. She did have a tiny nibble on my marshmallow, but that was all. She didn't really want it, but I said, "Go on, Mom. You've got to have a taste."

Maxine can't eat peanuts—she's mlergic to them. If she has just one tiny, weeny bit of peanut, she'll puff up like a balloon and be really sick. It's true. Mrs. Edwards told me. Maybe that's why Mom isn't here anymore. Maybe she was mlergic to marshmallows. She didn't puff up, she just slowly shrank thinner and thinner until one day she disappeared and wasn't at the hospital anymore. Maybe that tiny little bit I gave her was what started it all. She must be better by now. I just wish she'd hurry up and come home because I want to show her my new Furby.

Jamie was telling Vicky about his camp and how no one knew about it. I told Vicky about the ferny little den, but she just made a face and told us to forget it. She got up and started climbing down the ladder when Jamie stopped her.

"We've got to stay together, Vick," he said in a whisper. "What's going to happen to Rhi if we're not around?"

"I don't need Miss Sticky Slob Bottom, thank you very much," I said, but the words came out all wobbly.

"We could look after ourselves," Jamie pleaded, but

then Vicky said all snappy, "Oh, yeah? Great idea—just like last time."

"That wasn't my fault!" Jamie called after her, but Vicky didn't stop, she just ran to the house and slammed the back door behind her.

"It wasn't my fault, Rhi," said Jamie when she'd gone. "I didn't want them to take us away from Dad."

I remember when it happened. It was a long time ago. It was after Mom had gone. We'd all got home from school, and Dad was out driving a truck for Mr. McCready. Mr. McCready was so funny. When he came around to give Dad his money, he'd always look around first like his mom was going to pop out of the bushes and tell him off for doing something naughty. Anyway, that evening Jamie said he was fed up with jam sandwiches because Dad was never there to make dinner, so he said he would make us all French fries. Bossy old Vicky told him not to, but he didn't listen. I love fries, especially with loads of ketchup. He put the oil in the pan and turned the stove on and then there was this cartoon on TV, so we went and watched it for a while.

When we came back in the kitchen, it was full of smoke. I called Vicky, and she shouted at Jamie to come out and shut the door. Vicky had to go next door and get Mrs. Cantoni to call 911. Everyone on our street came out when the fire engine arrived. A bit later Mrs. Frankish turned up with a police lady and said we had to go with them.

When Dad came to see us in the first children's home, he looked different. His face was all rough and scratchy when I gave him a kiss. Jamie told him a joke. Jamie said it was really funny, but Dad never even laughed. He just sort of twisted his mouth up like he had a pain somewhere. When Jamie said, "Your turn," Dad said he'd run out of jokes at the moment. He didn't even smell like Dad anymore. He smelt of Jamie's gym uniform when it needs a good wash.

CHAPTER 6

Vicky

*I*t was starting to get dark when Mrs. Frankish went out to the tree house. I was in my bedroom waiting for Matt to arrive. Okay, so Cowpat-face wasn't going to let me go out, but she couldn't stop Matt from coming over to see me. I could hear Jamie shouting at her that she was an old bat and old bats weren't allowed in. Terrific. Matt was bound to turn up right in the middle of my embarrassing brother and my embarrassing sister screaming and yelling at my embarrassing social worker. What more could a girl want?

Mind you, nothing bothers our Mrs. Frankish. She just waited for a gap in between Rhianna's yells and Jamie's abuse, then called up that Paul was home and

28

they both had to go in and pack their stuff for tomorrow. Rhianna pretended she couldn't hear her, but of course old Frankenstein wasn't having it. She just gave her that look that she does. She takes a great big breath, makes her eyes go all slitty and looks down her nose at you like she's going to turn you into something slimy. No wonder Rhianna's convinced she's a witch. Jamie once told Rhianna that she's got a whole load of boxes in the trunk of her car. He said one day, when Mrs. Frankish was talking to Paul, he sneaked out and opened one. Inside there was a frog hopping around, and it was still wearing a little school uniform. He might be an annoying little brat, but he sure has got a great imagination. Ever since then, Rhianna's never argued with her for long.

I went downstairs and saw Paul sitting in the kitchen. Rhianna was asking him if Sarah liked her card, but he just looked at her as if he'd forgotten who she was or something. It was that same look Dad had the week before Mom died. He'd come home from the hospital and just sit in a chair for hours, staring at the wall like he'd been turned to stone. Then suddenly he'd start talking about all the mad, crazy things we were going to do together when Mom got better and came home. About two days before she died, Dad was going on and on about how we'd have a fantastic vacation together next summer. I couldn't stand it any longer. I yelled at him, "For goodness' sake, Mom isn't going to get better—she's going to die!" The minute the words were out, I wished I hadn't said them. But it was too late. He just looked at me for a few seconds, then the tears started rolling down his cheeks and he started sobbing really loudly. I didn't know what to do. He was supposed to be the grown-up, not me.

Mrs. Frankish made Paul a cup of tea and started spooning sugar in. Rhianna told her he didn't like sugar, but Mrs. Frankish kept on shoveling it in like it was suddenly going to make everything all right.

"I'll help you pack all your things, Rhianna," she said with a big, bright smile pasted over her face. "Paul just needs to have a few quiet minutes on his own."

"He still won't drink your stinky tea," Rhianna retorted.

They went upstairs and Jamie followed. I looked at Paul. I don't think he even realized I was there. I was scared to ask about Sarah. I was even more scared to ask about the baby. So I turned and walked out of the kitchen door into the backyard and took a big gulp of air. I staggered to a bench and sat down, feeling sick. I sat there for a while just trying to get my head together. Then I saw Matt coming along the road. It was too late to go in; he'd already noticed me and given a wave. I didn't want him to see me like this. I knew I looked like a mess.

"Hey," I said, trying to sound as casual as I could.

"Hi, gorgeous."

No one's ever, ever called me gorgeous before. He put his arm around me and drew me close to him. He was actually going to kiss me! My first proper kiss! I know it was wrong, with Sarah and the baby and everything, but for a few perfect seconds I just felt so happy. Wait till I tell Rosie, I thought. Forget about Romeo and Juliet. This was the real thing. Our lips were just about to touch—eat your heart out, Charlene Slackton—when suddenly I heard a yell from our bedroom window and I felt something land on my head.

It was a pair of Rhianna's underpants! Can you believe it! A pair of her disgusting navy blue underpants! I'll kill her! I thought. I will personally kill her!

Matt laughed and called up to her, but I was furious. How dare she! How dare she ruin my first kiss! Possibly the only kiss I was going to get for the next century, as I was about to be banished into the unknown. Something in me flipped, and I started yelling at her. I saw Matt look a bit taken aback, but I didn't stop. Now *I* was the embarrassing one for a change. It was like everything had bubbled up into one big gigantic mess and I couldn't keep the lid on it all anymore.

I hadn't thrown a real full-blown tantrum since I was about eight, but this definitely made up for it. Mrs. Frankish came out in a flurry.

"This is all your fault!" I screamed, throwing the underwear at her. "If you hadn't taken us away from Dad in the first place, we wouldn't be in this mess, packing up to go who knows where!"

She tried to say something, but I wouldn't let her, so she just stood there holding the underpants and going more and more red as I heard myself screeching at her more and more loudly. The nosy woman from across the street came out to have a look, but I still didn't stop yelling. I couldn't have stopped if I'd wanted to. And what's more, I didn't want to. Everything I cared about was going to be taken away from me. I had nothing to lose. I was going to yell like crazy—scream like a loony. Matt started to fidget, then he mumbled some excuse and said he had better get going.

"Matt," I said, "don't go!"

But he just gave me a wary sort of smile, then walked off down the road and out of my life. Watching him hurry away slowed me down. Suddenly I was drained. I had nothing left to say. He turned the corner and I burst into tears just as Paul came out. I heard him quietly say to Mrs.

Frankish that he'd manage now and she'd better head home. She didn't look too happy, but Paul insisted. She told him she'd be around the next morning to collect us. She patted his arm and then, still holding the underwear, got in her car and drove off. I looked down and saw I was shaking. It was really weird—I was shaking like jelly and I couldn't stop. Paul turned to me.

"Come on, love," he said gently. "Let's get you inside. It's cold out here."

CHAPTER 7

Rhianna

I ran into Jamie's room to hide from Vicky. I could hear her outside screaming. I didn't mean to make her so mad. I hid under Jamie's bed and put my fingers in my ears. I wanted the noise to stop, but it didn't, so I started screaming too. Jamie came in. He bent down and put his face under the bed.

"Stop it, Rhi!" he called. "Stop that racket right now . . . or I'll give you a double Chinese burn."

He does really nasty Chinese burns, so I stopped.

"That's better," he said as he got out his backpack. "Now, get out from under there."

I crawled out from under the bed covered in dust.

He opened his school bag and looked at me. "Now,

watch carefully because you'll have to pack your backpack too in a minute."

"What about the suitcase Paul gave you?" I asked.

"People don't carry suitcases around when they're running away. They need to travel light," he said. "With just the things they *really* need."

"Are we really going to run away?" I asked.

"It'll be fun."

I thought for a second. "What about Vicky?"

"Vicky's a big fat pain in the butt. We don't need her bossing us around all the time."

"No, we don't."

Jamie put in his warm sweatshirt, some jeans, two pairs of thick socks, his flashlight, his Spider-Man sleeping bag and his camping book.

"Right," he said, "now go and pack yours just with stuff you really need."

"Okay," I said, and ran quickly off to our bedroom.

I got out my backpack and piled in my Furby, my baldy Barbies, my Lava Lamp and Baby Emma with the poked-out eyes. Last of all, I put in the big photo of me, Vicky, Jamie and Mom and Dad. Great-Auntie Irene had taken it outside her house. She was really, really old and had cracks on her face like dried-up Play-Doh. The photo was a bit blurry. It looked like it was raining, but it wasn't—it was lovely and sunny. Vicky's got her eyes shut because she blinked, and you can hardly see Jamie because he crouched down behind Jip to keep him still.

Jamie came in. "You'll have to sleep in your sweater and jeans tonight," he said as he helped me roll up my sleeping bag and fix it on top. "And we have to do a secret commando raid to get some food and our water bottles."

He told me to go down and talk to Paul in the sitting room while he sneaked into the kitchen.

"What shall I talk about?" I asked.

"Doesn't matter. Anything will do."

In the living room Paul was talking to Vicky. She wasn't yelling anymore, just making funny sort of gulps. Paul gave her a tissue, and she blew her nose.

"How long will we have to be away?" Vicky asked Paul.

"I don't know," he said.

"It'll only be a short while, though, won't it?"

Paul still didn't say anything.

"We'll be back before Christmas, definitely. We will be back then."

Paul didn't answer.

Vicky looked at him. "Promise me we will."

"I'm sorry, Vicky . . . things change—I can't say because I just don't know."

Vicky made a funny snorty noise, then rushed upstairs saying she was going to pack her stuff.

I love Christmas. Vicky and Jamie don't believe in Santa, but I do. And I know how he gets down chimneys too. You know he's really fat? Ha! Well, he isn't, actually. All that fatness is just air. When he wants to come down a chimney, he just pulls at a string on his belly button and all the air whooshes out from his tummy and he goes really skinny. That's how he can slip down the chimney. Then, when he gets to the bottom and he's left all the presents, he pulls another string and blows himself up again like a balloon.

When we were little, Dad used to bring us presents when he came back from driving. Mom would get cross sometimes and tell him she needed the money to pay the bills, but he would just laugh. After Mom was gone, two men came around to take our beds and the sofa and armchairs back to the shop. One was really grumpy, and the other just kept saying he didn't want any trouble. When they'd gone, Dad said not to worry because every cloud had a silver lining. I looked outside to see, but they were all gray. Anyway, he'd found some money under the sofa, so he took us out to get dinner. We came back and sat on the carpet with the French fries on the paper in the middle like a big picnic. It was fun. Mom never let us do stuff like that. And he didn't get mad when I spilled my soda. He just said it didn't matter anymore because they'd be back for the carpet next week.

I heard Jamie in the kitchen banging around. Paul heard him too.

"Paul," I said quickly, "do you want to hear a joke?"

He looked around me at the kitchen door.

"It's the funniest joke ever, in the whole wide world," I said.

"Go on, then," he said. I looked at him. His eyes were really red and tired. Suddenly I wanted to cheer him up. I really, really did want to tell him the funniest joke ever in the whole wide world, but I didn't know how. You see, I don't actually know any jokes at all. Jamie tells me them all the time, but I get all mixed up and can never remember them.

It was a good thing that the next second Jamie came out of the kitchen. He gave me a thumbs-up sign and ran upstairs with a bag.

"Gotta go," I said, running out and following Jamie upstairs.

"Thought you were going to tell me the funniest joke in the whole wide world?" said Paul, calling after me.

"Nah," I said. "It's really boring."

CHAPTER 8

Vicky

I went to bed early that night. I'd packed my stuff and didn't feel like going back downstairs. Mainly I was kind of embarrassed about my whopping great tantrum earlier. I couldn't believe how I just lost it so completely. In front of Matt too. Errrch! I couldn't bear to think of it, but Matt's bewildered and wary expression kept flashing up in my mind's eye. He probably thought I was a real head case. Totally nuts. Maybe it's a good thing we're leaving tomorrow, I thought. At least I wouldn't have to face him at school for a while.

Paul had been on tenterhooks all evening in case the hospital called, but no one did, thank goodness. He called at nine, and the nurse said Sarah was comfortable, whatever that meant. Poor Sarah. She and Paul so wanted this baby. We all did. Rhianna and Jamie had already gone to bed. I guess they were as fed up as me. At least Rhi got her Furby and her cake. I looked over at her, snuggled up under the covers and fast asleep, an old teddy bear tucked in next to her. There was the faintest trace of a smile on her face; she looked like she hadn't a care in the world. The great thing about Rhi was she never stayed miserable for long. She lived in the present and never beat herself up over things she should have done or didn't do—they were in the past, and they just didn't matter anymore. And she never really worried about what was going to happen. She lived for the moment. That was all. Boy, was she lucky. When Mom died, I tried to soften it all for her. There I was launching into this big "Mom's gone but everything's going to be all right" routine, and when I finished, she just looked at me with those big gray eyes and asked if we could have ramen noodles for dinner.

I'd been furious with her earlier, but being angry with Rhi is like being angry with a puppy that's chewed one of your best shoes. Just one look at its trusting expression and you can't help but forgive it. Maybe this residential school wouldn't be so bad. And maybe, if I was with a decent family, they'd take me to visit or even let Rhi stay over some weekends. Maybe Sarah would get better really quickly and we'd all be back together for when the baby arrived . . . maybe everything would work out perfectly . . . maybe little pink pigs would learn to fly and take over the world. . . . Maybe. I was sick of maybes. Paul had said he didn't know when we would be coming back. "Things change." What exactly did he mean?

A really horrible thought rushed into my head, and no matter how hard I tried, I couldn't push it out. What if "I don't know" became "never"? Jamie was right. We'd be split up for good and powerless to do anything about it. I told myself to shut up. Sarah and Paul wouldn't let us down. They wouldn't. They cared about us. Wanted the best for us. But then, we had been let down so many times over the last two years. Promises, like balloons, had popped in front of our eyes. Mrs. Frankish was always saying that things are never as bad as you imagine. But it's all right for her—she has the imagination of a fruit fly.

CHAPTER 9
Rhianna

When I woke up, Jamie was standing over me with his finger on his lips.

"It's time to go, Rhi," he whispered.

I looked over at Vicky. She was curled up asleep in her bed. I didn't feel like going anywhere, but Jamie picked up my backpack and we tiptoed out so she wouldn't wake up. We crept down the stairs in the dark. The house was fast asleep. I couldn't see where I was going, so I grabbed Jamie's arm. I tripped over Vicky's shoes in the hall and banged my knee on the little telephone table. It hurt so bad I wanted to cry, but Jamie put his hand over my mouth to stop me. We put on our sneakers and coats. Then, really quietly, he unlocked the front door.

Out in the street it was quiet and still. The black cat from next door came up to us and rubbed his back around my legs. I gave him a quick stroke, and he stared at us. I bet he wondered where we were going. A car came up the road, so we hid behind the mailbox, but the man driving never saw us. Nobody did.

When we got near the woods, everything was even darker, so Jamie put on his flashlight. I don't think it was working too good because it only made a little tiny circle of yellow on the sidewalk.

"It'll warm up," Jamie said, but it didn't.

I don't like the dark. When we first went to Paul and Sarah's, they said we could each have our own room, but I didn't like the shadows that came at nighttime, so I used to creep into Vicky's bed and snuggle up next to her. She'd give me a hug and stroke my hair. If I shut my eyes tight, sometimes I could pretend it was Mom back home. In the end Sarah said that we'd better move my bed in and share the room so Vicky could get some sleep. Now my old room is painted ready for the baby, and there are lovely new curtains with rabbits and ducks on them, but I don't care—I'd rather be with Vicky.

The path down into the woods looked like a big black mouth.

"I don't like it," I told Jamie. "I'm not going down there."

"It'll be okay. Anyway, we'll be at the camp soon."

I wouldn't budge, so he got cross.

"We can't go back now, Rhi!" he said, taking my arm and trying to pull me in.

I was stronger than him. He couldn't make me, so in the end he started walking down the path into the woods on his own. I watched him go and then looked around. I didn't know which way to go. I wanted Vicky. She always knew what to do. Suddenly I heard a really scary noise. The shadow things were coming to get me now that I was on my own. They'd waited for Jamie to go off, and now they saw their chance. I screamed, then ran after Jamie as fast as I could.

When I caught up with him, he told me to stop bawling my head off or he'd whack me and then I would have something to cry about.

"But I'm scared of the monsters!"

He laughed. "I'm not! If any monsters try anything, I'll just give them a karate kick in their rudey bits, then finish them off by thumping them one."

Jamie's really brave. I'd just run away if there was a monster standing in front of me ready to pull my arms and legs off or suck out my blood.

It started to spit with rain, but Jamie said it didn't matter because when we got to his camp we'd crawl inside his den and be warm and dry like two snug bugs in a rug. He got out two granola bars that he'd taken from the cookie jar. He let me have the one with the red wrapper. The red ones taste the best. He said we'd have a competition to see who could make theirs last the longest. I won by loads.

I'd just finished the last little crumb when we got to the camp. It looked different in the dark. Some of the branches of the den had fallen in, and some had blown away. He said he'd fix it, and he started pulling them all off and piling them up on the roof again. It took him ages, and he kept swearing when they fell off. When he'd done it, we got out our sleeping bags, unrolled them on the floor of the den and crawled inside.

"I can smell dog pee," I said.

"Shut up, Rhi."

It was like lying on prickly hedgehogs, and my hands still felt cold. Jamie said he'd blow on them to warm them up. He made a funny *hhrrrrr* noise like a dragon blowing out smoke.

I was just falling asleep when Jamie jabbed me with his elbow. "Stop taking up all the room!" he hissed.

"I'm not taking up all the room!"

"You are, you fat lump!"

"I am not fat! Don't call me fat because I'm not fat!"

"Move over!"

He started pushing me. I pushed him back, so he gave me a whopping great shove right in my side.

"Stop it, you conkhog!" I yelled.

He shoved me again. Harder. I rolled into the wall. Some of the branches fell down on my head. Jamie started going balloony.

"You're trashing my den!"

"It's a lousy den!" I yelled back at him. "You said we'd be as snug as bugs in a rug!"

Then we heard the noise outside.

"It's the monsters, Jamie!"

"Shush!"

"With stabby beaks."

"Shut up, Rhi!"

"They can stab their way through branches."

"Rhianna! Put a cork in it!"

"You've got to do something!"

But Jamie didn't get up. He just wriggled down in his sleeping bag till I could only see the top of his hair.

Then he said in a funny wobbly voice that he wasn't going anywhere.

"But you said you'd do karate kicks if any monsters came. You promised!"

"Will you shut up!" He sounded really cross. I told him it wasn't my fault the monsters were outside waiting to bite off our heads. Jamie hissed if I didn't shut up straightaway, he'd bite off my head himself and save the monster the job of it. I started asking him how because he hasn't got pointy teeth but then we saw something coming toward us.

Jamie picked up one of the branches. He crawled out and started to wave it around his head. He didn't look very scary, and his arm was shaking.

"Quick!" I screamed. "Kick it in its rudey bits!"

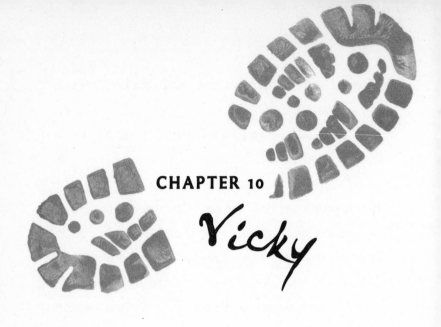

CHAPTER 10

Vicky

Just you try it, Jamie Davies!" I shouted, shining my flashlight on him. "And put that stick down before you hurt yourself!"

"What are you doing here?" asked Jamie.

"I've come to take you home."

"Oh, yeah?" said Jamie. "That'll be interesting. Seeing as we don't have a home at the moment."

"Jamie and me have run away," said Rhianna. "And now you can too."

"I'm not staying." I said, avoiding Jamie's eye. "You've both got to come back."

"Why? Who's going to miss us?" he muttered. "No one wants us now. Can't you see that, Vicky? We're just in the way, that's all. More paperwork for Mrs. Frankish."

"What about Dad?" I said.

"What about him?" asked Jamie, making a face.

I looked down at the ground and kicked at some leaves.

"Maybe he wouldn't want you to run away," I said awkwardly.

"So why doesn't he come home and look after us?" asked Rhi.

"I'm sure he would if he could, but—"

"Yeah, 'cos we're the refugees now," interrupted Jamie fiercely.

"It might not be easy for him to get away. He can't just drop everything and . . ."

But Jamie wasn't listening anymore. He'd turned around and walked back to the shelter.

"I'm not going, and you can't make me," he muttered as he crawled back inside.

I looked at Rhianna. "Come on, Rhi. If we go back now, we won't get in trouble. No one'll even know we've been out." I took her hand in mine. It was freezing.

"Okay." She grinned. "If you come to my new school with me."

"I can't, Rhi. They won't let me."

"I'm not going without you and Jamie."

"It might not be that bad, Rhi. They've got a pool. You love swimming. And you'd make lots of new friends, and it won't be forever. . . ." My voice went all funny. Like I was fighting with the words and they were winning. I stopped and turned away.

"What's the matter?"

"Nothing," I snapped. "I've got something in my eye. That's all."

I couldn't do it. I couldn't pretend anymore that when we were split up it was only going to be for a while. It was all a big fat lie, and I knew it. I'd known it when I'd packed my backpack (just in case) and followed Jamie and Rhianna out the front door and down to the woods. Deep down, I knew I wouldn't be coming back. Jamie was right. We weren't wanted. I just hadn't wanted to admit it. Not out loud.

When we first started school, the authorities thought Rhi could manage without any help, but every morning at the school gate, Mom would whisper to me, "Keep an eye on your sister, Vicky." So I did. I looked out for her. Kept the bad kids away. Protected her from danger. Every single day. And now that Mom was dead, I would always have to look out for her. Forever and ever. Amen. I took a deep breath.

...

"So let's see this fantastic den," I said quietly, a few seconds later. With a big grin on her face, Rhianna took me over to the entrance and pulled me in. It looked like a bit of a mess. Ten to one it was chock-full of creepy crawlies too. Ugh! I hate things like that. I took off my backpack and pulled out my sleeping bag.

"I thought you wanted to go 'home,'" said Jamie in his "I won, so there" voice.

"I'm not leaving you two here on your own," I said, unrolling my sleeping bag and laying it next to Rhianna's. "Anything could happen."

CHAPTER 11

Rhianna

When I woke up, everything was green. It was like being in the Emerald City in *The Wizard of Oz*, except it was cold and the top of my sleeping bag was all damp. I bet Dorothy didn't have a soggy sleeping bag. I bet hers was all nice and cozy and warm. Something tickly was crawling in my hair, and I could hear Jamie and Vicky laughing somewhere. Then I remembered. I wasn't in the Emerald City, I was in Jamie's little den in the woods. We'd really done it. We'd really run away together. I wriggled out of my sleeping bag and crawled outside.

"Welcome to Camp Fun," said Jamie in a funny fancy

voice when he saw me. "And would Madame care for some breakfast? I'm afraid we're all out of cereal."

"Good!" I said. "Cereal is pantyhose."

"But we do have a bag of the finest jam doughnuts."

He brushed some mud off the bag and opened it. Yippee! I love doughnuts. Things were getting better and better. (I bet Dorothy didn't have jam doughnuts.) I put my hand in and pulled out a lovely, squishy, jammy blob.

"There's two and a bit each," said Vicky, pulling out another one. "And there's milk to drink." She sniffed the carton, then took a big swig. Milk dribbled down her chin.

"Vicky, you mucky mess pup!" I laughed.

"Who cares?" said Jamie. "This is *our* camp. We can do what we like. There's no rules, no adults to boss us around and no worries!"

"No worries! No worries! We've got no worries!" I grabbed Vicky's arm, and we danced around and around, laughing and giggling.

Suddenly we heard a noise. Someone was coming. Vicky quickly pushed me back into the den and dived in after me. "Don't make a sound!" she hissed in my ear.

Jamie pushed his way in, and we sat there all in a tumble. What if it was Mrs. Frankish? She would be so cross she'd turn us all into frogs. I didn't want to be a frog.

I hate frogs. This wasn't how running away was supposed to be. Jamie said we weren't going to have any worries. I started crying, and Vicky put her hand over my mouth. We listened for a few seconds. Someone was outside walking around. A face appeared at the little doorway.

Vicky and I screamed, but Jamie laughed. It was his friend Sam.

"I was going to knock for you, like we said yesterday, but they're going nuts back at your house. There's a police car and everything."

"A police car! Awesome!" said Jamie.

"It is not awesome," snapped Vicky. "It's terrible. Think what Paul must be going through."

"What's going on?" Sam asked.

"Sarah's in the hospital," Vicky told him. "They can't foster us anymore. We were going to be split up, so we came here."

"I'm not going back," said Jamie.

"I know," I said. "Maybe we could call Paul up on Vicky's cell and tell him we're okay but we've just run away."

"Great idea," said Jamie. "The minute we do that, they'll find us."

"They'll soon find you anyway," said Sam. "They're

going to do a search—I heard the policeman telling some woman."

"Mrs. Frankish," said Vicky.

"She's really a witch, Sam," I said. Someone had to tell him.

"Oh, yeah?"

"Yeah. She'll probably get her broomstick out and fly over us like in *The Wizard of Oz*," I said, feeling all shivery.

"Don't you worry, Rhianna—we'll just chuck a load of water over her and she'll melt into a trail of green slime."

"Thanks, Sam." I liked him.

Vicky looked up. "We can't stay here. We've got to go somewhere where they won't be able to find us. Somewhere far away. Somewhere we'll be safe."

"Where's that?" I asked.

"I don't know, but if we don't get going right now, we won't have a chance."

She started stuffing my things into my backpack. "Rhianna, what on earth is all this?" she exclaimed, picking up one of my baldy Barbies.

"Jamie told me to take all the things I needed. So I did."

"I give up," sighed Vicky, shoving my Barbie into my bag.

"Watch my Furby!"

She picked up the photo Great-Auntie Irene had taken. Jamie looked at it.

"That's it!" he shouted. "We'll go and stay at Great-Auntie Irene's."

"But she's really old," said Vicky. "Mrs. Frankish said we weren't allowed to live with her."

"So? We can help her with chores and things she can't do anymore—carry heavy shopping bags and take Jip for long walks for her. It's perfect!"

"How are we going to get there, Jamie?" asked Vicky. "She lives miles away out in the country. Don't you remember the trip there, with you throwing up all the time and Rhianna asking if we were nearly there so many times that she drove Dad bonkers? Anyway, how much money have you got?"

"Twenty pence."

"Rhianna?"

"Nothing."

Vicky put her hand in her pocket and brought out some money. "Forty pounds. Our birthday money. That won't get us far."

"I've got an idea," said Jamie, stuffing his sleeping bag back in his backpack. "Get your things together. We've got to hurry."

Sam helped me bundle the rest of my stuff into my backpack, but Vicky was getting cross because Jamie wouldn't tell us where we were going. When we were all ready, he just said, "Follow me!" and charged off at a hundred miles an hour.

CHAPTER 12

Vicky

"Jamie! Sam! Slow down. Wait for us!" I didn't like to yell in case someone heard us, but it was still early, and luckily we didn't meet anyone. Jamie led us out the far side of the woods, through a maze of back roads that eventually took us right out of town and to Mr. McCready's depot. There were a few trucks parked inside the yard, which was edged with rusty iron railings.

We watched from behind some bushes. The place was pretty quiet. Too early for McCready, the old crook. When he came to our house once, I overheard him asking Dad to make some "special deliveries." Maybe Dad didn't realize the stuff was all stolen, I thought suddenly. Maybe Dad was completely innocent and had just ended up being the fall guy . . . huh. Who was I kidding? Dad must have known full well what he was doing.

There were a couple of drivers in the Portakabin. I could see them inside, laughing and chatting and swigging their tea before they set off on their routes. I recognized one of them. It was Pete, one of Dad's old friends from years back. He was all right. Used to give us fruit gum. He carried around big packs of it because he was trying to give up smoking. Pete drove the northern route, always covering the same territory and always dropping in to see his "old mom" on the way. Then it clicked. I understood Jamie's plan. Pete's mom lived about thirty miles away from Great-Auntie Irene—one year Pete had even made a detour to her house to deliver some Christmas presents from us.

If we could just get onto his truck, he'd unknowingly take us most of the way for free. Perfect. I grinned at Jamie, who was looking pretty pleased with himself.

"Not bad, you little tyke," I said. "Come on."

Carefully we climbed up and over the railings into the yard, then scuttled toward the parked trucks. But which one was Pete's? I hadn't a clue. If we got on the wrong one, it would be a disaster. We could end up anywhere. Suddenly Rhianna started jumping up and down excitedly.

"Shut up, Rhianna!" I hissed at her.

"It's this one!" she said, pointing to a red truck with a battered knitted teddy bear tied to the grill at the front. "Remember?" she asked. "Pete told me his name's Lucky."

Inside the cab on the dashboard we found three full packs of fruit gum. Rhianna was right. This was definitely Pete's truck.

As quickly and quietly as we could, we went around the back. Pete's teddy bear was bringing us luck too— the doors were unlocked. We scrambled in and said our good-byes to Sam. Jamie made him swear he wouldn't tell anyone where we were going. He promised and closed the doors after us. We groped our way forward in the semidark, sat ourselves down behind some cardboard boxes and waited.

About ten minutes later, we heard the doors being rattled and locked and then the sound of Pete getting into his cab. We heard him start up the engine and felt a sudden lurch forward as the truck pulled out of the depot.

We'd done it. We were on our way. Jamie gave me a thumbs-up, and I grinned back at him. We were together, the three of us, and maybe everything was going to be all right.

We got out our sleeping bags and quietly made ourselves as comfortable as possible. I was petrified Pete might hear us, so we sat in silence to start with, huddled together, listening to the drone of the engine. After a while we became a bit more confident and started talking in whispers about all the things we were going to do when we got to Great-Auntie Irene's. A couple of hours passed, and the journey dragged on. Jamie and Rhianna fell asleep, one after the other, which was probably a good thing as they wouldn't feel sick. About another two hours later, I was just beginning to doze off when I felt the truck pull to a halt. Maybe we're at Pete's mom's, I thought.

Quickly, I woke Rhianna and Jamie. We waited, hardly daring to breathe, as we heard the doors at the back of the truck open. From our hiding place we could hear Pete rearranging some of the boxes near the doors. I looked over at Jamie and saw to my horror he was making really strange faces. What on earth was he playing at? Now wasn't the time for silly games. Suddenly I realized. He was trying to stop himself from sneezing.

All at once, he let out an enormous "Ahhhh-tishooo!"

"Hey! Who's in there?" Pete called out roughly. "Come on—show yourself. Get out of there now!"

There was nothing we could do. We all stood up.

"Pete?" I called. "It's only us. Neil Davies's kids."

"Neil's kids?" He lowered the crowbar he was holding. "Vicky, isn't it?"

"Yeah. It's me and Rhianna and Jamie."

"What are you all doing in my truck?"

"Running away," Rhianna chipped in before I could stop her.

"Jamie, go and help Rhianna a minute," I said as I quickly jumped down from the back of the truck and pulled Pete to one side. I glanced around. We weren't at his mom's at all. We were at a highway rest stop next to a service station.

"Pete," I said, "we're in trouble. We really need your help."

"Where's your dad, then? Haven't seen him for ages."

"Working abroad," I lied. I could feel my cheeks burning. "We're just going to stay with some relatives for a bit. We needed a lift."

"Sure," said Pete quietly. "Look, the truck's full of apples. Go and help yourself. I just need a break for five minutes or so, then we'll get going."

He walked to the cab, and I dashed back to Rhianna.

"Where's Jamie?"

"Said he wanted to stretch his legs. Is Pete cross?"

"No. Everything's going to be fine," I told her. "We're going to be okay!"

She'd already gotten into the apples. I told her to go easy, or she'd end up with a bellyache. Just then Jamie appeared from around the other side of the truck.

"Why's Pete talking about us?"

"What?" I asked.

"On his cell."

My stomach lurched.

"Quick! Get your stuff," I hissed.

We snatched up our bags. I looked around desperately. Which way? Beyond the rest stop, cars and trucks were roaring up and down the highway. All around us were people, stretching their legs, eating lunch, exercising their dogs and taking a break from their journeys. The rest stop was surrounded by a deserted stretch of scrubby woodland. Our only way out.

"Come on." I grabbed one of Rhianna's hands, and Jamie grabbed the other. Then . . . we ran. And ran.

CHAPTER 13

Rhianna

Vicky and Jamie pulled me along so hard my arms hurt. I yelled at them to stop, but they wouldn't, even when I said I felt sick.

"You shouldn't have eaten all those apples, Rhi," said Vicky.

"I didn't eat them all, I only had five. There were boxes and boxes left."

Vicky wouldn't tell me where we were going. I thought we were going to get back in Pete's truck and ride in the front with him like I did once with Dad, but Vicky said we couldn't. She always spoils everything.

I was still feeling sick when we ran out of the woods and came to a road. I wanted to stop, but Vicky said we had to keep going. But I didn't want to, so I started crying. Vicky was shouting at me and Jamie was trying to pull me along when this car stopped. The lady driver rolled down the window and asked if we were okay.

"Fine, thank you," Vicky told her. "We're just going back home. . . . Um . . . we're a bit late. Our mom hates it when we're late."

I looked at her. She was going bright red like a tomato.

The lady had short curly gray hair and nice orangey lipstick, and she looked a bit like my teacher, Mrs. Edwards. "Well, if you're sure. . . ." She looked at us for a long time, but then she drove off.

We carried on, but Vicky said we'd better not run anymore, in case people thought we were in trouble or had done something wrong. So we walked really quickly. It was just as bad. I asked Vicky if we could have spaghetti for dinner and soda to drink, but she said no, so I said what are we having then, and she said she didn't know.

We came to a crossroads, but Vicky didn't know the places on the road signs or which way to go. Jamie said we needed a map. Vicky told him they didn't grow on trees and that we'd have to find a shop or something. But we didn't even know which way to go to find a shop. Vicky decided we should go straight on for a bit because the other roads were just lanes and she said there wouldn't be any shops down little lanes. So we went straight on along the main road for ages, but she was wrong. We didn't see any shops at all.

Vicky got out the last doughnut and said if I walked without making any fuss, I could have it. I said okay. It was all squashed, and the jam had squirted out. I gobbled it down in one gulp, and I was still hungry.

We went up a hill, and when we walked down the other side, we saw a small gas station by the side of the road.

"They might sell maps in there," said Jamie.

"I'll go and find out," said Vicky. "Stay here, behind these bushes."

I watched her walk into the gas station shop.

"Keep your head down, Rhi!" Jamie pulled me down behind the bush.

"Ow! You don't have to pull my arm!" I told him. I was cross. "See how you like it."

I pushed him, and he fell back onto the ground.

Then Vicky came back. She looked cross.

"Rhianna! What are you doing?"

"He started it!"

"For goodness' sake!"

Jamie got up and gave me a bad look. A Chinese burn look. I went and stood behind Vicky.

66

"All right. I've got a map. Now let's try and figure out where we are."

Vicky said we'd better keep away from the main roads just in case anyone was looking for us. She unfolded the map and looked at it for ages with Jamie. I asked her if we were nearly there and she said not far, but we had to walk a few miles until we got to the train station. At the station we had to get on a train, and when we got off the train, we had to walk some more. I was tired. I didn't want to walk anywhere, but going on a train was all right. That sounded like fun.

"Come on, Rhi—if we keep going, we'll soon be at Great-Auntie Irene's," said Jamie.

"Can we have spaghetti when we get there?"

"I expect so."

"With cheese on top and no mushrooms in the sauce?" Mushrooms are yucky.

"Course we can," said Jamie. "And we'll have a massive breakfast tomorrow—bacon and eggs and toast and jam and hot chocolate and muffins with chocolate chips. And Great-Auntie Irene'll make us lovely dinners every single night . . . roast dinners too, like Mom used to."

"With dessert afterward?"

"And second helpings. Thirds if we want."

Vicky laughed.

"We will!" said Jamie.

"Why not?" said Vicky with a shrug. "Great-Auntie Irene's a fantastic cook."

"Can she make pizzas, then?"

"With her arms tied behind her back juggling a squirrel on her nose," said Jamie.

"Really?"

Jamie laughed. "Course she'll be able to make pizzas, Rhi. Don't worry."

"And if she gets tired of cooking, I can make cheese straws for her," I said. "I'm good at them."

It was all going to be lovely. I couldn't wait. I started walking faster.

"Slow down, Rhi!" called Vicky.

"No. You hurry up—I want to get there!"

CHAPTER 14

Vicky

*I*t was hard work keeping up with Rhi. For a start, she's miles taller than Jamie and me, and when she gets into her stride, she really gets going. She wasn't moaning about being hungry anymore—she was talking nonstop about all the fun we were going to have when we got to Great-Auntie Irene's.

We reached the crossroads and turned left down the lane, following the directions from the map. I felt happier now, out of sight and away from the traffic of the main road. We tracked our way through the lanes for about an hour before taking a right fork into the narrowest lane so far. Grass was growing through the pavement down the middle, and Rhianna and Jamie were playing a game jumping from clump to clump. About half an hour later, we rounded a bend and found ourselves at a dead end, standing in front of two huge wrought-iron gates. They were closed, blocking our route. Through the gates was a long tree-lined driveway, dotted with crumbling, mossy statues on pedestals. On either side of the gates were high stone walls topped with spikes.

"What do we do now?" asked Jamie, climbing on one of the gates and swinging it forward and back. It squeaked painfully.

"Get off there, Jamie."

He carried on swinging. I checked the map, then looked down the tree-lined driveway.

"I don't understand it. The station's over that way. We must have taken a wrong turn somewhere."

"I'm not going all the way back—it's miles and miles."

"The road we want comes out on the other side of the grounds. But we can't go that way—it's private property."

"Who says?" Jamie jumped off the gate and started walking down the potholed driveway, kicking the loose gravel as he went. "Come on. It's our 'private' shortcut."

I hesitated. To me those huge gates, high walls and sharp spikes were all shouting "keep out" pretty loudly. "We better not."

But Jamie wasn't listening, and Rhi was already trotting after him down the long driveway. The pair of them were zigzagging from statue to statue, inspecting each one and sniggering at the more scantily dressed ones.

I looked around. Everything was so neglected I wondered if anyone even lived there anymore.

"Hey, Vicky, this one's 'armless!" Jamie was standing behind the stone torso of a woman, waving his arms around as Rhi giggled uncontrollably.

I weighed the risk. If we just ran through and out the other side, likely as not, no one would see us—no one would even know we'd been there. On the other hand, if we went back all the way we'd come, we'd have a huge detour. Jamie and Rhi were both in a good mood now, but that wouldn't last forever. They were tired and hungry. And so was I. I made my choice, shoved the map back in my backpack and ran after them. I caught up with them as they were looking at a statue of a woman with wild snakelike hair and a manic look on her face. Moss was growing out of her left nostril.

"Hey, Vicky—it's you!" Jamie quipped.

"Very funny." I glanced at the statue again and couldn't help but smile. It had more than a passing resemblance to Charlene Slackton, I thought.

CHAPTER 15

Rhianna

At the end of the driveway there was a big old house. When we saw it, Vicky made us walk behind some bushes and creep along so if there was anyone inside and they were looking out of the windows, they wouldn't see us. It didn't look like a very friendly old house. On each side of the front door was a stone lion staring at us with its front paws stretched out. One of them only had one ear. I started counting the steps up to the door, but Jamie said I'd better be quiet or the lions would come to life and eat me. Vicky said he was just making it up and told him to shut up. I stopped counting the steps.

Three big birds were sitting on a low roof at the end of the house. They weren't made of stone—they were greeny blue with long, feathery tails. One of them swooped down near us making a squawky noise. I jumped behind Vicky.

"It's all right, Rhi. They're only peacocks. They won't hurt you."

I still didn't like them. Another one flew down and they both started pecking the ground near us. Their tails were so long they dragged on the ground behind them. Suddenly one of them lifted its tail up and spread it out like a big fan. The feathers had yellow and blue and green eyes. It was beautiful. Mrs. Edwards helped us make fans at school when it was hot. It's quite difficult because you have to fold the paper one way then you turn it over and fold it the other way and then back the other way and so on until it looks like stairs when you open it out. I helped Maxine because she can't do folding. Some of her fingers don't work. They're twisted up. She can do coloring, so we spent ages decorating them. Mine was purple because that's my favorite color. It didn't have eyes on it, but it did have some glitter that was left over from when we did snow pictures at Christmas. Mrs. Edwards stapled the bottom edge for us so it made the fan shape. We took them into the playground at break time, but Charlene Slackton snatched them from us and squashed them into balls and threw them down the toilet, and everyone laughed except me and Maxine and Mr. Harris the janitor, because they got stuck down there and he had to put his special gloves on to get them out.

There was green stuff growing on the house. Vicky said it was ivy. It was everywhere. All over the walls and the roof. It was even growing over one of the lions' backs and up the front door and on some of the windows, covering them up. The rest of the windows were very small and dark with diamond shapes on the glass. It looked like the sort of house an evil old witch would live in.

"Maybe Mrs. Frankish lives here."

"Don't be silly, Rhi. We're miles and miles away from home. It would take her hours to get to work every day."

Not on her broomstick, I thought.

"I don't think anyone lives here anymore," said Vicky.

I wasn't sure about that. I looked up at one of the windows and saw a curtain move. "Look, there she is!"

"Rhi—stop it!"

"But Mrs. Frankish was peeping out from behind that curtain!" I pointed up at the window. Some of the glass was missing and the curtain was blowing to and fro.

"It's just the wind, Rhi," said Vicky. "There's no one there."

"This place is really creepy," said Jamie. "Let's get out of here."

CHAPTER 16

Vicky

The house and gardens must have been truly beautiful once. A real paradise. Now it was a sad sort of place, forgotten and neglected. As we made our way around the nettles and brambles that stung and scratched us, I kept having a weird feeling that we weren't alone; someone or something was there with us, aware of every move we made.

I felt better when we went past the house and came out into a large area of knee-length grass. In the center was a huge pond choked with water lilies and weeds.

"Wow!" Jamie shouted excitedly, leaning so far forward he looked as if he might fall headfirst into the pond any second.

Swimming under the canopy of water lily leaves were several enormous fish. Each was at least a foot long. We sat down on the edge of the pond and watched them.

Jamie reached out his arm and trailed his hand in the water hoping the fish would come over to him.

"Watch they don't nibble your fingers off," I joked.

It was Rhianna who heard them first. "What's that?" she asked.

Jamie and I strained to listen. Then I heard it too. It was the sound of dogs barking excitedly. It quickly became louder. A lot louder. They were coming in our direction. We barely had time to scramble to our feet before they emerged from the bushes on the other side of the long grass: two huge and powerful dogs bounding toward us. Rhi screamed.

"It's the lions!"

They stopped a few meters from us, staring threateningly, with their ears pinned back, their teeth bared and their tails stretched out but not wagging.

"Go away!" shouted Jamie, waving his arms at them. "Get lost!"

One of them started to growl, low and menacingly. I wasn't sure what to do, but I knew we were in trouble. Dogs like these could be vicious. I'd read stories in the papers. They could injure. They could even kill.

"I don't like them!" Rhi wailed. "I don't like them!"

Before I could stop her, she'd turned to run.

"Stay where you are!" an authoritative voice called. A white-haired woman dressed in a light-blue raincoat tied at the waist with a piece of string emerged from behind one of the bushes.

"It's all right, Rhi. Do as she says. Stand still."

Rhi looked at me, terrified, but did as she was told.

Then something odd happened. I'm not sure what the woman did—I didn't actually see her do anything or say anything—but the dogs suddenly stopped growling. One even started to wag its tail—not a friendly "I'm pleased to see you" wag but a slow, suspicious, "So who are you, then?" wag.

"Now, very slowly walk over to me."

We did as she said. The dogs made no attempt to follow us, and once we were behind the woman it seemed as if they had lost interest in us. They bounded off, disappearing back in the bushes.

"Are you all right?" she asked.

Jamie and Rhi nodded, but then, unable to stop myself, I burst into tears.

"You'd better come inside. I'll make some tea. Best thing for nasty shocks." She took one of my nettle-stung hands in her own knobbly arthritic one and felt it with the other. "And I suppose we'd better find something for those stings."

Without another word, she turned and started walking back toward the house, stopping by a large clump of nettles.

"There's probably some dock leaves growing nearby," she told us. "If you pick them and rub them on your skin where you've been stung, it'll help."

I looked down and saw a clump of large green leaves. I picked a couple and handed them to her. "Are these the ones?" I asked.

She held them close to her face. "That's them," she said.

We rubbed the leaves over our stings, and it was lovely to get some relief from those painful white bumps.

"Those mutts don't belong to me, more's the pity. Be far better trained if they did. The people down in the lodge own them." She waved her hand to indicate their direction. "Too lazy to walk them. Let them roam free in my grounds. My brother would have had words with them." And with that, she turned and we went into the house.

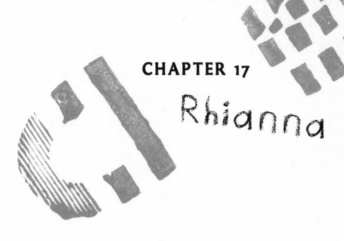

CHAPTER 17

Rhianna

I wasn't sure I wanted to go past the lions into the old lady's house, but Vicky said it would be all right. We went up the steps. Jamie patted one of the lions on its head and climbed up on its back.

"Nothing to be scared of, Rhi. They're just stone. They won't bite. They won't do anything."

"But you said—"

"I was only teasing."

I went past them quickly and through the front door.

The hall was full of old furniture. On the walls were paintings of people in long-time-ago clothes and piles of books and boxes of papers and the biggest piano I'd ever seen and a clock in a big case like in the "Hickory Dickory

Dock" nursery rhyme. Everything was dusty. I don't think the old lady liked cleaning up much. I don't either. I'd much rather play with Baby Emma or my Barbies.

We went into the kitchen. There were saucepans hanging down from a rack over an old stove and a white sink with a green stripy curtain around the bottom of it, a big table and chairs. The old lady picked up the kettle, filled it and put it on top of the stove.

"I suppose you're hungry too," she said.

"I'm starving!" I told her. "We've only had doughnuts and apples today."

"Doughnuts! Good grief. . . . Is that what your parents feed you?" She shook her head, then went over to the fridge. She opened the door and took out some shiny trays like takeout cartons.

I was just about to tell her that it wasn't our mom or dad that gave us the doughnuts when Vicky started talking very loudly and Jamie told me to shush.

"It's very kind of you," said Vicky all politely. "We don't usually have doughnuts. . . . They were . . . a treat."

"Well. That's something. You're growing. You need decent food." The old lady looked down at the trays and sniffed. "Meals on Wheels. Not exactly high cuisine, but I don't know what I'd do without them." She picked each tray up and, putting it close to her eyes, read the labels on the tops. "I've got cottage pie, toad in the hole and . . . pasta."

"Pasta, please!" I said quickly. I didn't like the sound of the other things.

"But we can't eat your food," Vicky said.

"Yes, we can. She said we could!" I butted in quickly. I was starving.

The old lady laughed. "It's quite all right, my dear," she said to Vicky as she put the trays into the oven. "Marion'll be around tomorrow afternoon to drop off more. I'll just tell her I was hungry this week. She'll be very pleased. She's always saying I've got no appetite. . . . Now, my brother—he's a different kettle of fish. He could eat a horse and still have room for dessert."

"Eurgh. I wouldn't eat a horse," I said. "Even if I was really, really hungry."

The old lady laughed, but I meant it.

CHAPTER 18

Vicky

The old lady had been named Elizabeth Margaret after the queen and her sister. When she was a child growing up during the Second World War, her family had to evacuate this house, because it had been too dangerous to stay so near the city with all the bombs and air raids every night. She and her brother, Lionel, hadn't wanted to leave their parents or each other, but they'd had no choice. So, at the age of twelve, armed with a little box containing her gas mask and a small suitcase of clothes, she'd taken the train to the countryside of Devon with the rest of the girls and teachers from her school. Her brother was sent to Canada on a ship called the *City of Benares*. It left Liverpool docks on September 13, 1940, with ninety children on board. By then Elizabeth was already in Devon. Lionel was just ten—the same age as Jamie.

As we sipped our tea, she took down from a shelf an old brown tin with "Sharpe's Toffees" written on it in gold lettering. It was full of curled, faded photos of her and her brother taken before the war.

"We were pretty much free-range at your age. Especially in the school holidays. Out after breakfast, back when it got dark. Exploring, usually. Every day with Lionel was an adventure."

We looked through the photos together. They were happy, smiling pictures, taken at the seaside or on picnics or at Christmas. Lionel was almost as tall as Elizabeth, with blond hair, suntanned skin and a cheeky wide-mouthed grin.

"Well, this won't get the baby bathed," said Elizabeth with a small sigh, getting up briskly. She went over to the oven. As she opened the door, heat filled the kitchen, which she wafted away with her frail birdlike arm.

"As ready as they'll ever be," she said as she slowly took out the foil containers and put them on the table. She told us where to get the plates and cutlery, and I served up the food while Rhi and Jamie laid out the knives and forks.

We sat around the table and ate hungrily as Elizabeth poured herself another cup of tea and sipped it slowly.

I tried to say as little as possible about us, but it was difficult. Elizabeth wasn't nosy or anything. It wasn't that. She didn't keep asking questions. In fact, she didn't really ask many at all, but there was something about her. Something that made me let things slip. Things I wanted to keep hidden. I told her we hadn't meant to do anything wrong, we'd just got a bit lost and were taking a shortcut through her grounds. She just nodded as if this sort of thing happened every day. Then it came out that we were heading for the train station because we were going to our great-aunt's house. Somehow, maybe because she'd told us all about being evacuated, and because Jamie was the same age as her brother when he was put on that ship to Canada, I started explaining about us being fostered and how we were going to be split up. She was quiet for a moment. I thought she was getting ready to tell us we'd better go straight back home. But she didn't.

"It's a terrible thing for a family to be separated. Not knowing whether you'll ever see people you love again," she said softly.

We helped clear away the plates, and I washed them up in the big stone sink. Jamie and Rhi wiped them dry and placed them back on the shelves.

Then Jamie asked if we could explore the house. I could tell he'd been itching to do this since we'd come inside.

Elizabeth smiled. "It's not looking its best," she said.

"We don't mind," replied Jamie, and he was off in a flash.

It was a huge and rambling mansion just like the one from *The Lion, the Witch and the Wardrobe*, with long dark passages, heavy antique furniture and old tapestries hanging from the walls. There was even a suit of armor, which freaked Rhi out but enthralled Jamie, who was desperate to try it on. I put my foot down and told him no. My friend Rosie would have had a field day. There were nine bedrooms upstairs, two with four-poster beds complete with heavy moth-eaten curtains draped around them so they looked like huge holey tents. Every single room had its own fireplace, even the big old bathroom with its huge rusty-edged bath and cracked black and white tiles.

We were just about to go back downstairs when we saw a small door at the end of the passageway.

"Wonder what's through there," said Jamie, quickly diving around the door. I followed him in and gasped. It was a boy's bedroom—the most amazing boy's room ever.

Laid out on the floor against the walls of the room ran a miniature train track complete with model bridges, tunnels, buildings, trees and people. Spaced around the track were about ten different engines, each with an assortment of carriages and each one a detailed intricate replica of the real thing. On the chests of drawers there were models of ships, including a battleship, a pirate ship with sails and skull and crossbones flag and a passenger steamer with a big wheel attached to its side.

Hanging from the ceiling were models of old-fashioned airplanes, all covered in a film of dust, but every one carefully made and painted. It was like Jamie had died and gone to heaven. He didn't know what to start with first.

We didn't hear Elizabeth come in.

"This is Lionel's room," she said softly. "He built all those planes himself."

Jamie had already picked up one of the trains and was examining it.

"Will he mind if Jamie touches his stuff?" I asked quickly.

"Of course not," she replied.

I looked around for Rhianna. She'd disappeared. Out in the hallway there was no sign or sound of her. I felt a slight twinge of panic.

"Rhi?" I called.

There was no answer.

"She won't have gone far," said Elizabeth as we

started checking all the upstairs rooms. "Don't worry," she added, realizing I was getting anxious.

"You wouldn't think we were twins," I told her. I explained that Rhi had been starved of oxygen when she was born. "Nothing's easy for her. She can't manage on her own, so I sort of have to help her with stuff."

The old lady looked at me with her cloudy pale blue eyes. "Her time will come."

I didn't understand. Rhi wasn't suddenly going to get a new brain, and I didn't believe in miracle cures. So what did she mean?

We eventually found Rhi in one of the spare bedrooms in the four-poster bed, curled up and fast asleep under a beautiful golden silky eiderdown. On the pillow next to her lay a small china ornament about three inches tall. A black and white penguin with a cheeky smile and a pink bow tie.

I leaned forward to take it, but Elizabeth stopped me.

"It's all right. Don't wake Sleeping Beauty," whispered Elizabeth with a smile.

It did seem cruel to wake her. I glanced out of the window. It was beginning to get dark. We should have left hours ago. The peacocks were screeching as they prepared to settle down for the night. I wondered if the dogs were still loose. I thought I could hear them barking in the distance. The garden was a tangled mass of black shadows. Anything could be lurking out there. I wasn't looking forward to leaving—I was dreading it.

I didn't want to be the one in charge anymore, sorting everything and everyone out. I just wanted to be an ordinary thirteen-year-old kid with no decisions bigger than whether to buy a teen mag or a bar of chocolate.

I sighed. I felt completely lost.

"You can stay here tonight if you think that's best," said Elizabeth.

I nodded. Relieved.

"Thank you."

Elizabeth hesitated, then took my hand in hers.

"Come with me. I want to show you something," she said.

We went downstairs into the living room. There was a dusty old desk in the corner of the room. She pulled out an old paper folder. Inside was a single, yellow, slightly mildewed newspaper cutting. She handed it to me. It was dated September 28, 1940. There was a black-and-white photo of the ship the *City of Benares*.

I looked at Elizabeth. She gave a small firm nod. I read on. The ship had been torpedoed by a German submarine six hundred miles out at sea.

"Only thirteen of the ninety evacuee children

survived. And my brother wasn't one of them. He never got to Canada, and he never came home." Her voice was full of sadness. "There's not a single day goes by that I don't think about him." She looked me in the eye. "Vicky, I'm an old woman. Lots has changed since I was your age. But some things stay the same and are always important— brothers and sisters . . . families. You have a choice about what you do. You can choose to go on . . . or you can go back. It's up to you, and I can't tell you what's best. But there's one thing I will say: desperate times call for desperate measures."

CHAPTER 19

Rhianna

It was funny waking up in Elizabeth's house. It was cozy and warm in the bed. I didn't want to get up. I wanted to stay under the lovely silky yellow cover, but Vicky was already up and putting on her sneakers.

"Come on, Rhi, time to get out of bed," she said.

"I don't want to. I'm tired." I picked up the little penguin on my pillow and stroked its shiny head.

"We've got a train to catch. The sooner we get going, the sooner we get to Great-Auntie Irene's."

"But I'm really, really tired."

"You can have a big sleep when we get to Great-Auntie Irene's. You can sleep for a whole week if you like!"

"I want to sleep now."

Vicky sat down on the edge of the bed and looked at me. "Don't you remember how much you loved it when we were there on vacation?"

I nodded.

"Well, it's going to be like that but even better. Because we're going to live there, it'll be like we're on vacation all the time."

"Really?"

Vicky nodded. "Every single day," she said.

I got up out of the bed and pulled on my sneakers. A vacation every single day. I liked that idea.

Jamie was already downstairs with Elizabeth. He was eating cornflakes.

"All set?" Elizabeth asked, looking at Vicky.

Vicky nodded and grinned. "Thank you," she said. "For everything." She gave Elizabeth a hug.

"You've got a good head on those shoulders. I know you'll use it. Your great-aunt is a very lucky woman."

We picked up our backpacks. I still had the little penguin in my hand. I held it out to Elizabeth.

"This is yours," I said.

"Keep it," she said with a smile. "He might bring you luck."

"Thank you," I said. I popped him into my coat pocket and zipped it up so I wouldn't lose him.

We all walked down the road behind the house, past a little stream. There were more statues and another set of big gates. Next to one of the gates was a little house. Elizabeth said this was the lodge. Inside we could hear dogs barking.

"It's all right," Elizabeth told us. "The owners lock them up during the day while they're out."

She told us how to get to the station, and we all said good-bye, and she hugged us and then watched us walk off down the road. I looked back after a while. She was still there. She was very small, like a little bird. She gave us one last wave and then we went around the bend and we couldn't see her anymore.

It took a long time to get to the station. Vicky showed me where we were going on the map—it didn't look far, but it took ages. I was getting fed up and wanted to sit down and have a rest, but bossy old Vicky said I couldn't. She said we had to keep going.

I'd never been on a train before. At the station the man behind the glass gave us our tickets and said, "Enjoy your trip." Vicky and Jamie went over to the board to check what time our train was. I sat down on a bench to wait for them and took my penguin out of my pocket, but then this man came up and sat down next to me.

"Hello," he said. "That's a nice little penguin."

"I know," I said.

"Do you like animals?" he asked.

I nodded.

"So do I," he said. "But I like real ones best. I've got some lovely puppies back at my house. They're only a few weeks old. I don't suppose you like puppies, though. . . ."

"Oh, yes . . . I love them," I said.

Then Vicky came over. I don't know why, but the man got up and hurried out of the station and down the street. Vicky took my hand and pulled me toward the bathroom.

"But I've just been, Vicky!" I told her, but she still rushed me in there.

"I'm not a baby. I don't need to go every two seconds," I told her.

She didn't take any notice. She just started filling up our water bottles from the tap. "You mustn't talk to anyone, Rhi, not a word!"

"You can't tell me what to do—you're not Mom. Anyway, I was only doing a conversation. Mrs. Edwards says doing a conversation is a Life Skill."

"I don't care what Mrs. Edwards says!"

"I'll tell her you said that."

Vicky made a groaning noise. "Forget about Mrs.

Edwards," she said. "Come on. The train'll be here any minute."

I was really cross with her. She was always bossing me around. I went back into one of the stalls and sat down on the seat.

"Rhi!" she yelled. "Come on."

I didn't budge.

"What's the matter now?"

"I'm not talking to you," I said. "And I'm not doing anything you say. So put that in your nuckets and boil it."

CHAPTER 20

Vicky

"Rhianna!"

"I can't hear you. . . ." She started singing to herself in the bathroom stall. Something told me this wasn't going to be easy.

Outside on the platform I could hear our train being announced. What if Jamie got on and we were left here?

"Rhianna, you've got to come, right now. I mean it!" I could hear my voice getting tighter and tighter, and her tuneless singing getting louder and louder. She was so infuriating sometimes; I could throttle her. I knew I couldn't force her out onto the train—she was much bigger and stronger than me—and if I tried, she'd throw a tantrum. There was only one thing to do. It was going to be a gamble, but I had no choice. I took a deep breath and fought hard to keep my voice sounding light and unconcerned.

"Okay, Rhi. You stay here. That's fine. I'm going on the train with Jamie." I turned to go. "Bye, then. . . ."

The singing faltered slightly, but I knew I had to call her bluff. I kept on going, resisting the temptation to turn around. Outside on the platform there were crowds of people waiting.

I rushed up to the train, my palms sweating and my heart pounding. I looked behind me. No sign of Rhi. Jamie appeared at the window inside one of the cars and grinned.

"Where's Rhianna?" he mouthed through the glass.

I felt sick. The panic was rising. How could I have been so stupid to leave her on her own in that bathroom? What was I thinking of, and what on earth was I going to do now? I tried to motion to Jamie to get off the train, but he thought I was telling him to put his bag on the luggage rack and turned away. People streamed around me, but I was rooted to the spot. I just didn't know what to do. Who should I go after—Rhi or Jamie? In a few more seconds, the train doors would close and the train would pull away, taking Jamie with it, but if I leapt on, it would mean leaving Rhi on her own, and that didn't bear thinking about. But would Jamie know what to do if the train went off without us? He wasn't the most clued-up kid in the world.

I started to bang on the window. A man in a beige suit turned and glared disapprovingly at me. I smiled apologetically, and he tutted and shook his head, muttering to a woman in a green coat. At this rate, we'd be discovered any second, but I had to do something. Ignoring the man, I started thumping frantically on the window again. Suddenly I felt a hand on my shoulder and froze.

I turned around, expecting to be confronted by an angry conductor, but to my relief, I saw Rhi standing in front of me, her face blotchy and red.

"Don't ever do that again!" I snapped, yanking her hand off my shoulder. She reeled back as if I'd hit her. Tears started to roll down her bewildered face.

"I'm sorry. Vicky. I'm sorry."

She was shaking, and so was I. I put my arm tightly around her and bit my lip till I could taste blood. "It's okay. Don't cry anymore."

The conductor blew his whistle as the last few passengers got on. I hurried Rhi onto the train and looked for Jamie. He was standing at the end of the now-crowded car.

"What took you so long?" he asked, staring at me accusingly.

Most of the seats were taken, so we made our way into the next car. Rhi had finally stopped crying but was hiccupping noisily. She wouldn't let go of my hand, and in a way, I didn't want her to.

Eventually we found a table between four seats. A man with a beard was sitting in the far corner. He had a little radio, which was playing a cricket match. I hate cricket, it's sooooo boring. He obviously thought so too because his eyes were shut and he was snoring loudly. We sank down in the three spare seats and, for the first time that day, I allowed myself to relax.

I looked out of the window while Rhi chatted happily with Jamie, her tears forgotten. We drank the water from our bottles—it tasted disgusting, but we were all so thirsty we didn't care anymore. We were on our way, whizzing out of the town.

Gradually the countryside became wilder and fields and woods loomed in the distance. The rhythm of the train seemed to be saying, "You're nearly there, you're nearly there."

Guiltily, I thought of Paul and Sarah. It was horrible not knowing what was happening. Please, please, please let their baby be okay. I imagined them in the hospital, Paul sitting by Sarah's bed waiting for her to wake up, or for the doctors to come around, or encouraging her to eat something. I knew the routine. I'd done it with Mom. I hoped they were too caught up in their own troubles to worry too much about us. An uncomfortable thought struck me. Dad would know we had run away by now too. What would he be thinking?

I forced myself to think of something else. Matt. No. Rosie? I desperately wanted to text or call her, but I'd deliberately kept my phone switched off. I knew the police could trace calls. It was much too risky.

I shut my eyes and decided that I had to think positive. To look forward, not backward. When we got to Great-Auntie Irene's, she'd be surprised to see us of course, but she'd give us something good to eat and tell us everything was going to be all right from now on and I didn't need to worry anymore. She might be really old, but she had all her marbles and she'd sort everything out. When we were first taken away from Dad, Mrs. Frankish had asked if we had any other family who could look after us. There was only Uncle Mac or Great-Auntie Irene. Uncle Mac runs a sheep farm somewhere in Australia, and Mrs. Frankish said we weren't going there. When she found out Great-Auntie Irene was eighty-one and didn't have a phone, she said staying with her wasn't an option, and we weren't to bother her.

I should never have listened to the old bat—Great-Auntie Irene was family.

It really would be like a fantastic vacation, I thought. Better, even. It would be like coming home. A proper home. And, if we could never go back to Paul and Sarah's, it wouldn't be the end of the world. We'd make a new life, start new schools and make new friends—no one like Rosie, maybe, but she was a one-off. Rhi would improve leaps and bounds with Great-Auntie Irene's help. She loved reading stories with her. And Jamie would settle down at last. He'd finally stop whacking people. He was always so gentle with Great-Auntie Irene's dog, Jip—that dog brought out the soft side of him. And we'd help her too—earn our keep with the chores like shopping or cleaning. Even Rhi could help wash up or set the table, so us being there would be good for her too. And we'd be company.

"Old people get lonely," Great-Auntie Irene told me once. "We like to have you youngsters around to shake things up a bit and remind us we're still alive!"

I thought of Elizabeth back in her huge mansion with just her memories for company. We could go back and see her. Visit. Take Great-Auntie Irene. They'd get along great. They'd be swapping wartime memories like there was no tomorrow. I smiled to myself. Everything was going to be perfect.

I opened my eyes. Rhi and Jamie were playing tic-tac-toe on a scrap of paper. Jamie was letting her win for a change, and she had a big grin on her face. The radio was still on, but the cricket seemed to have given way to the news. I double-checked our map, mentally ticking off the stations we'd already stopped at and planning our route when we got off at the station after the next one. Suddenly something the man on the radio said made me sit up sharp.

". . . the three missing children, nonidentical twin girls aged thirteen and a boy of ten . . ."

I froze. Jamie and Rhi hadn't heard. The man began to describe our exact appearance. Hardly daring, I glanced over to the people sitting on the other side of the aisle. They were chatting and laughing at the moment, but how long would it take one of them to notice us? I quickly reached over and flicked the radio off. The man with the beard immediately started to stir.

"Quick, get up," I urged Jamie and Rhianna.

"What's the matter?" asked Jamie.

The man picked up his radio, puzzled at its abrupt silence. He shook it, then realizing it had been turned off, glared at us and switched it on again even louder, giving us another rude stare.

"Appeals for the children to return home have so far been unsuccessful and police are becoming increasingly concerned for their welfare and safety. And now the weather. . . ."

Jamie went white and grabbed his bag. I got Rhi to her feet and started ushering her out of the car following Jamie. We passed a woman in a red sweater who glanced up at the three of us.

There was a flicker of surprise in her expression. She looked as if she was about to say something, but I didn't wait around to listen; I bundled Jamie and Rhi into the next car. The train was coming into a station.

"What's the matter, Vicky?" Rhi asked.

"We've got to get off now, Rhi. Right now."

"But we've only done five stations. I counted. You said six."

"Never mind. Come on. Bring your bag."

We moved quickly through the cars to the other end of the train, and when it stopped, we leapt out.

It was a tiny station surrounded by countryside in the middle of nowhere, with large pots full of bright red geraniums and a white picket fence. It was very quiet and completely deserted except for a few hikers in shorts and walking boots, who got off at the same time as us.

I looked back at the train—the woman in the red sweater was on the platform talking urgently to the conductor and pointing at us. She had recognized us, all right. The conductor was torn between moving the train off and chasing after us. As we ran to the exit tumbling through the group of hikers, she called after us, "Come back!" but we didn't.

We were nearly at Great-Auntie Irene's. We were nearly there. We couldn't give up now.

CHAPTER 21

Rhianna

When we ran out of the station, Vicky made us hide in some bushes so she could have a look at the map again. She said because we got off the train early it was going to take us a bit longer to get to Great-Auntie Irene's. We went down a footpath. There were no houses, just fields and hedges and trees and lots of sheep with muddy bottoms that baaed and clattered away noisily if we went near them.

We walked for ages and ages, and the brambles scratched my legs, and my feet were sore, and I kept tripping up and banging my knees when we climbed over gates. Then it started raining and my hood wouldn't stay up so my hair got wet and water trickled all down my neck and I wanted to go back to Elizabeth's house. I told Vicky, but she wasn't listening because she was looking at the map and arguing with Jamie about which way to go. Then Jamie said we had to watch out for adders. One little bite, and our mouths would start foaming and our arms and legs would jerk and we would die if we didn't get the right medicine.

Once in class, one of Maxine's arms and legs started jerking and she had foamy spit coming out of her mouth. I don't think it was an adder bite, though. We've only got guinea pigs in our classroom. They're named Floppy and Tom, and I don't think they're poisonous. Mrs. Edwards didn't say what it was. She didn't say anything, except we all had to go out into the hallway and wait. I didn't want to because I saw Maxine looking at me, and I knew she wanted me to stay with her and hold the hand which wasn't jerking, but they wouldn't let me. An ambulance came. Even Charlene Slackton stopped laughing and stared with her mouth open when they put Maxine in the back. It was break time, and everyone was watching. They turned the siren on and all the seventh-grade boys chased the ambulance out of the gates. Maxine didn't come back to school for ages.

I was fed up with running away. So was Jamie. He snatched the map out of Vicky's hands and said she was just a stupid girl and everyone knew girls couldn't read maps. He looked at it for ages and ages, and when Vicky said, okay, where are we then, he threw it back at her and said how should he know.

Vicky was really angry because she didn't catch the map when he threw it at her. It fell on the ground and got all wet and muddy and then it started to blow away and she had to chase it and when she caught it, it was ripped.

She told Jamie off, but he just shouted really, really rude words at her and told her he didn't care.

My jeans were all covered in mud and I was cold and my socks were soggy. I told Vicky, but she said it was all right because we'd be there soon. But we weren't. We just kept on walking. And walking. And walking.

When my class did the sponsored walk to raise money for our own computer, we never walked this far. It was sunny and we had drinks and snacks, and Mrs. Edwards played I Spy with us as we went along, and we sang songs and it was fun.

I kept asking Vicky if we were there yet, and she kept saying "in a little while" or "nearly," but we still weren't, and after a while, she stopped saying anything at all when I asked her. Jamie told me to shut up moaning or he'd give me a double Chinese burn and whack me. Vicky still didn't say anything, so I sat down on the wet grass. Then she said something.

"Rhi, what are you doing?"

"I want my dinner."

"We haven't got any dinner. Come on, get up!" She bent down over me and tried to pull me up.

I pushed her off.

"Get up!" Vicky shouted.

"What's the point?" Jamie said, chucking his backpack onto the ground next to me. "This is stupid. We don't know where we are—we could be going anywhere! We're probably going round and round in circles, thanks to you!"

"Me? You were the ones that wanted to run away!" Vicky snapped at us. "I never wanted to go anywhere, remember? This was all your big idea." She stared down at us both sitting on the grass in the rain. Her orange hair was frizzing up, and some was stuck to her face. "Get up! We've got to keep going!"

"Stop bossing us around!" yelled Jamie back at her. "We're fed up with it, aren't we, Rhi?"

"Yeah. You're always bossing us. We don't like it."

She looked at us both, then made a funny sort of gulping noise.

"Bossing you around?" she said. Her face was all red, and her mouth was twisted up. "Okay. That's fine. I'll stop bossing you around. Stay right here, if you like. It's not my job to watch over you. I'm not Mom. Understand? I'm not her." She wiped the wet hair from her face. "And something else. I'm tired and I'm hungry and I'm soaked to the skin too. I've had enough. So from now on you can do what you like. So I won't be bossing either of you around anymore because, guess what? I'm going back. And I don't care what happens to us all. They can split us up. They can send me to the moon. I just don't care anymore. . . ."

As she started to walk away, Jamie got up and ran at her, growling like a bear. He jumped on her back, and she tried to push him off. They fell on the ground, whacking and shouting and screaming at each other.

The noise stabbed into my ears and screeched around inside my head till it hurt. I shouted at them to stop, but they wouldn't, so I started yelling too. I ran off up the hill. I kept running up and up until my legs wobbled underneath me and I started falling, slipping and tumbling down I didn't know where.

CHAPTER 22

Vicky

*J*amie and I both heard the scream. Startled, we looked up, our fight forgotten.

"Rhianna!"

There was no sign of her. We ran full steam up the hill. Reaching the peak, we hardly dared to look down the other side. The ground fell away sharply and the steep slope was studded with trees, rocks and bushes. And then we saw her at the bottom, close to a boulder-filled stream. She was lying on the ground like a limp rag doll. We rushed down the slope, half sliding, tearing our clothes and grazing our skin. I could feel the panic rising. We were miles from anywhere. What if she were seriously hurt? Suddenly I felt sick. What if she were dead?

I stopped and stared at her. She was so still. Her face was splattered with dirt but white as chalk. Was this how dead people looked? I never saw Mom after she died. One evening she was in her bed at the hospital, the next morning she was gone and Dad was clearing her things out of the little locker. He'd said Jamie was too young and Rhi wouldn't understand but I should go to the funeral with him. But I just couldn't bear to see the coffin with Mom shut up inside it, so I never went. I never said good-bye.

Jamie got to Rhi first. He bent down close to her face.

"She's breathing," he whispered. "Vicky, don't just stand there. . . ."

But I didn't know what to do. This was my worst nightmare, and it was all my fault.

"Vicky!" Jamie shouted. "Do something!"

I pulled off my jacket, made it into a cushion and tucked it under her head. I got some tissues from my backpack, wet them in the stream and gently wiped the mud and dirt from her face. After a few seconds, her eyelids fluttered a little.

"Rhi, are you okay?"

She opened her eyes and groaned.

"Where are you hurt?" asked Jamie.

"Everywhere."

"It's all right, you're going to be all right." I looked at Jamie. His face was as pale as Rhianna's. He looked like he was going to cry.

Slowly, bit by bit, we got her to move each finger and toe, each arm and leg. Nothing was broken, and the worst of it seemed to be cuts and bruises, but she was exhausted.

"We've got to get her out of this rain," I said.

I looked around. The opposite slope was steeper, and a small waterfall cascaded down it into a fern-edged rock pool. A little way past the waterfall, some rocks jutted out. Thinking this might give us some shelter from the rain, I pointed it out to Jamie, and he went over to investigate. He disappeared out of sight for a few seconds, then reappeared with a grin on his face.

"It's a cave! It's half covered up with bushes and it's not very big, but it's dry inside. Someone's used it as a den before—there's stuff still in it."

We helped Rhianna up and managed to get her to the cave. We carefully pulled back the bushes and the branches of a huge wild rosebush with pink flowers.

Inside, there was a dusty matted rug on the floor and even a couple of moldy cushions. We sat Rhianna gently down on the floor, took off her wet coat and jeans and wrapped her sleeping bag around her. On a little rocky shelf there was an old cookie tin and some comic books. Everything looked as if it hadn't been touched for ages. Carefully, I opened the tin. Inside there was half a packet of stale cookies. We were so hungry we ate every last crumb.

I used some of the water from the stream to clean up Rhi's cuts as best I could. Then we unrolled our sleeping bags and gently zipped Rhi into hers.

"Rhi," I whispered as I snuggled her down, "I'm sorry. Those things I said. I didn't mean them. I do care about you both. Honest."

She looked at me with those big gray eyes, then asked, "Are you going to leave us here on our own?"

"Course not, silly," I replied, giving her a big hug.

"I'm not silly."

"You're right," I told her. "I'm the silly one."

After hanging up our wet coats and jeans to dry as best we could, Jamie and I lay down on either side of Rhianna, and within a few minutes, she was fast asleep. Ten minutes later Jamie was asleep too. It had been such a long, horrible day. I turned over and shut my eyes, but sleep wouldn't come. It wasn't quite dark yet, but the rain had stopped. As quietly as I could, I unzipped my sleeping bag, pulled on my spare jeans and wet sneakers and clambered out of the cave.

It was very quiet and the ground smelled fresh and earthy. I followed the path of the stream down through the woods, thinking that I could easily retrace my steps as long as it wasn't too dark. The woods were strangely silent. The air was misty, and the leaves on the trees were shiny and dripping. I followed the stream for about ten minutes and was just about to turn back when the trees thinned and the ground became more pebbly. I looked up and gasped when I saw it. Our island on the lake. Right in front of me. We'd been so close but hadn't even realized it was there. The lake was as beautiful as I remembered— the surface of the water shimmered pinks and oranges in the sunset.

I hurried down to the shore and looked up along the lake edge. Perched halfway up a hill was the house where Great-Auntie Irene lived with Jip. It sat with its green paintwork and gray tiled roof like an old friend patiently waiting for us. This was going to be our perfect new home.

I wanted to shout and whoop and cry all at the same time, but I didn't dare. In the distance, I could hear the high-pitched whine of a couple of dirt bikes. There were still people around.

It was late now. I didn't want to give Great-Auntie Irene a fright this time of night. She was an old lady and probably didn't get many visitors.

I heard Jip bark excitedly a few times as some quacking ducks splash-landed on the lake. I didn't feel like going back to the cave, I wanted to sit looking at the house and the lake and the island all night, but it was almost dark and I knew I must. The last thing I needed now was to get lost or lose my footing and fall over, so slowly and carefully, I retraced my steps back along the stream to the cave. Jamie and Rhi were still sound asleep.

"We're here," I whispered quietly into the darkness. "We really are here."

CHAPTER 23

Rhianna

In the morning, Jamie said to hurry and get up because we were going to see Great-Auntie Irene, but when I got out of my sleeping bag my legs felt all wobbly and tired. My jeans were nearly dry, but I didn't feel like hurrying anywhere, even to see Great-Auntie Irene and Jip, but Vicky said I'd probably feel better in a little while and gave me a drink of water from her bottle. She checked my cuts and bruises and kept asking me if I felt dizzy.

We followed the stream. I nearly fell in because it was slippery, and Vicky and Jamie had to help me. After a while we came out of the woods and could see the lake. Jamie and I started to cheer and shout hurray until Vicky said we had to be quiet, just in case. I wanted to go down to the water, but Vicky said, "No, look." She was pointing to Great-Auntie Irene's house. I felt so happy I forgot I was tired. We ran along the lake edge until we saw a path.

"Come on," Jamie said. "It leads straight to the house, remember?"

We were nearly at the bottom of Great-Auntie's yard when we saw the back door open and a lady come out. She had curly black hair and dark brown skin.

"She looks like Maxine's mom!" I whispered to Vicky.

"Must be a visitor," she said. "Or maybe it's someone who helps out with chores or something."

"She won't need her anymore with us around," I said.

A tall man with yellow hair followed her out of the house carrying a large cardboard box.

"Who's that, then?" I asked.

"They're robbing her," said Jamie. "Come on!"

He climbed over the gate and into Great-Auntie's back garden as the lady and man walked around the side of the house. Jamie started running.

"Jamie, wait . . ."

Vicky and I followed him, but by the time we got to the house, the burglars had got into a red car and were driving off.

"They've probably tied her up. We've got to help her," yelled Jamie.

We went up to the back door. Vicky slowly pushed it open. It creaked like doors always do in scary films.

"Great-Auntie Irene?" she called quietly.

There was no one in the kitchen. The house was quiet. The kitchen looked different. Great-Auntie Irene used to have a big cupboard with shelves on top with lots of pretty cups and plates and a big brown teapot and two china cats with a photo of us lot between them. It had all vanished like magic. Instead of Jip's old basket, there was a big furry cushion on the floor.

"Where is she, Vicky?" I said. "I want Great-Auntie Irene."

The door to the hallway started to open—Great-Auntie Irene had heard us at last.

But it wasn't her. It was a boy. A tall boy with tan skin and jumpy brown eyes.

"What have you done with Great-Auntie Irene?" said Jamie, going up close and sticking his face into the boy's. The boy stepped backward.

"Nothing. . . . Who are you?"

"We're her relatives, and we've come to see her."

"I don't know what you're talking about." His voice went all shaky. "This is my house—you'd better get out before my parents get back, or—"

"But she lives here."

"No she doesn't!"

Then Jip came bounding through the kitchen door.

"Jip!"

Jamie knelt down and gave him a big cuddle. Jip licked him excitedly.

"His name's Max."

Jamie moved over to the other side of the kitchen and said, "Jip!" The dog ran to him.

"See? His name's Jip. He belongs to our auntie."

"Max," called the boy. The dog turned and bounded back. "I found him just after we moved in. He was hanging around outside the back door, pawing and whining to come in. He was half starved and his coat was all matted." He looked at Vicky. "Mom thinks he must have belonged to the old lady who lived here before us."

"So where is she now?"

The boy pushed his shoulders up and down.

"I think she died. . . ."

CHAPTER 24

Vicky

I sank down on a nearby chair.

"Where's Great-Auntie Irene?" Rhi asked.

"She's not here, Rhi. She's dead." I said quietly. Rhianna started to cry.

Jamie kicked the table and thumped it hard with his fist.

"It's not fair!"

"D'you mind—" the boy started, but Jamie swung around and glared at him. Warily, the boy took another step back. He looked about my age or a bit older, but Jamie was pretty scary when he was angry.

"So what are we going to do now?" Jamie asked.

I sighed. I didn't feel like stating the obvious. It was

all over. Finished. We'd have to go back. Rhi would go to the residential school, and Jamie and I would be farmed out with strangers. We probably wouldn't see each other for months.

The boy was glancing nervously at Jamie, as if he might bite him at any moment.

"So . . . what's going on?"

I looked at the boy. Perhaps there was a way. Maybe this wasn't the end of our adventure.

"Can you keep a secret?" I blurted out.

The boy shrugged, puzzled. "Course."

"Don't tell him anything," snapped Jamie.

"My name's Daniel."

I looked at him, and suddenly the doubts rose up in me. Could I trust him? His eyes darted warily between us, as if he was expecting trouble. Then I remembered what Elizabeth had said about desperate times calling for desperate measures. I made my choice.

"We've run away."

Daniel turned and stared at me. I could feel myself going bright red. His face suddenly changed, his eyes opening wide. "You're those Davies kids, aren't you? I saw your pictures on TV last night. Everyone's looking for you."

"We're not going back."

"My mom and dad'll be home any minute."

"They mustn't see us. They mustn't know anything about us."

"But—"

"We've found a cave—" started Rhianna.

"That's my cave!"

"It's ours now," Jamie interrupted, glaring at Daniel fiercely.

Outside there were sounds of a car drawing up.

"Will you help us?" I begged him. "Please. . . ."

He looked uncomfortably from Jamie to me to Rhianna.

The doors of a car slammed. Rhianna started to wail loudly and embarrassingly.

"Not now, Rhi, for goodness' sake!"

"But I don't want to go to that school. I want to stay with you and Jamie."

The boy looked at her. Something had helped him make his decision.

"Okay . . . I'll help. But you'll have to be quick—and quiet."

Rhianna stopped her noise, and he led us through the hall and into the living room. Quickly, he unlocked and opened the French windows.

"Daniel?" a woman's voice called from the kitchen.

"Coming!" He turned to us. "Stay at the cave. They don't know about it. No one does. I'll bring you some food and stuff as soon as I can."

Before I could stop her, Rhianna dived forward and threw her arms around him in a big bear hug. "Thank you!"

The boy grinned, and for a moment, his sad eyes lit up and he looked like a different person.

Quickly he unhooked himself from Rhianna. "Just don't mess up my cave, all right?"

As Rhi nodded, Daniel's mom called him again from the hall.

"Now go!" he urged, hurrying us into the yard.

CHAPTER 25

Rhianna

Daniel brought us tons of food—pork pies, bananas, blueberry muffins (my favorite), cheese, bread rolls, potatoes, milk, orange juice and loads of other stuff. Yum. He even brought plates, cups and some knives and forks and spoons.

We were so hungry, but do you know bossy old Vicky made us wait till we'd swept out the cave for spiders and put our sleeping bags out over the bushes to get any bugs out.

We made the cave really cozy—Daniel and Jamie pulled the floor rug outside, and we each held a corner and waved it up and down and banged it with our hands, and a big cloud of dust came out of it, making us sneeze and cough. When we couldn't get any more dust out of it, we took it back inside the cave and spread it out on the floor again. We put all the food and the plates and stuff up on the shelf. There was room for my little penguin, my Furby, my baldy Barbies, Baby Emma with the poked-out eyes and my Lava Lamp too. I was glad I brought my lamp, even though there wasn't anywhere to plug it in. Vicky's flashlight didn't work anymore, but Jamie said I could borrow his and shine it behind the lamp. I picked some of the pink flowers and put them on the shelf too in a cup with some water. I put the photo of us all next to the flowers, then I gave Baby Emma a bath in the stream and put her outside the cave on a bush to dry in the sunshine.

We had pork pie and bananas for breakfast. Vicky said it wasn't really breakfast because it must have been nearly lunchtime, and when we'd finished, we were still hungry, so we ate all the muffins too.

"Beats school lunch," Jamie said, doing one of his megaburps. Vicky told him off for being disgusting but then Daniel did an even bigger burp. Jamie looked impressed. No one can do burps louder than him. Not even Ollie Stanmore.

But Vicky didn't tell Daniel off for burping. She didn't say anything at all.

"You haven't told Daniel off," I said, but she wasn't listening. She was just smiling at Daniel like I wasn't there or something.

"Vicky, you haven't told Daniel off. Tell him off too, or it's not fair on Jamie."

She made a face at me. Her eyes went all big and staring.

"Why are you making that face?" She still didn't answer, so I asked Jamie, "Jamie, why's Vicky making that funny face?"

Jamie shrugged. "P'raps she's trying to do a burp and it's got stuck halfway." He started laughing.

Daniel looked at Vicky. She stopped making the funny face and looked down.

"In some countries it's really rude if you don't burp," he said really quickly. "Means you think the meal was bad."

I tried to do a big burp too, but it came out wrong. Everyone just laughed, and Jamie said I sounded like a frog with a sore throat.

"What's your school like?" I asked Daniel. He didn't say anything for a bit, then he just poked the ground with a stick.

"I don't go to school anymore," he said really quietly.

"Everyone goes to school," I said.

"I don't."

"So what makes you so different?" asked Jamie in his "watch out or I'll whack you" voice.

"My mom and dad teach me at home. They're allowed."

"I bet," said Jamie.

Jip went up to Daniel and nuzzled his leg. He got up. "I'm taking Max down to the lake," he said without looking at us.

CHAPTER 26

Vicky

We followed Daniel down to the lake. There wasn't anyone there. That was what I'd loved when we'd stayed at Great-Auntie Irene's—we hardly ever used to see a soul, just the occasional boat puttering by or a few hikers. Most people stuck to the other shore, where the road ran all the way along the lakeside up to the town.

It was calm and sunny today, with no wind to ripple the dark velvety water. Upside down, near the water's edge lay Great-Auntie Irene's old dinghy. It looked even more battered and forlorn than ever, with its paint flaking off like old scabs and its name—*Guinevere*—half rubbed away. Poor Great-Auntie Irene. I couldn't believe that we would never see her again.

"Vicky, look!" called Rhianna, plonking herself down on its upturned hull. "Mom used to sit here by this boat and watch us play, remember?"

"Yeah. Mind you don't fall off."

"I won't. Don't fuss."

I bit my lip. Fussing was easier than remembering. Jamie looked on enviously as Daniel threw Jip a stick. Jip bounced eagerly into the lake, creating splashes of white spray and then swimming back with the stick in his mouth, just his head visible. He laid it at Daniel's feet, shook himself madly, drenching him in rainbow droplets, then looked at him as if to say, "Well, hurry up, throw it again!"

It was scorching hot. I sat down on the upturned boat next to Rhi, and we took off our sneakers and socks. Our feet were dirty, and mine were blistered.

Gingerly, we tiptoed over the grass and stones down to the water's edge. I dipped a toe in and drew back with a big gasp, but a little detail like ice-cold water was never going to put Rhi off.

"Come on, Vicky, don't be such a conkhog! It's lovely and warm."

"It's freezing!" I squealed. But Rhianna didn't care. She was already paddling merrily in.

"Vicky, let's play Monster Feet!"

I looked over at Daniel, who was watching us. I could have died with embarrassment. Monster Feet was a game we used to play in our old kiddie pool when Mom was alive.

Basically it consisted of stomping flat-footed in and out of the pool with our arms outstretched, making daft noises. It could last anything from five minutes to an hour, depending on Rhi's enthusiasm. I glanced at her. She was already getting into her role, sumo wrestler style, lurching and swaying from one foot to the other and growling softly.

"Rrrrrrrrrrrrrrrhhh!"

I sighed. It looked like we were in for a long session. . . .

Suddenly Jamie rushed past us. He'd pulled off his T-shirt, socks and sneakers and rolled up his jeans. With a loud whoop, he crashed into the water, then turned and started splashing us. Rhi screamed and tried to run away from him.

"Jamie, stop it! Daniel's mom and dad might hear us," I snapped.

"They've gone out," said Daniel, who called to Jip to come out of the lake.

"Thought they were supposed to be teaching you," teased Jamie as he got ready to give us another almighty soaking.

"Shut up, Jamie," I said, looking at Daniel, who was glaring coldly at him.

"Shut up yourself," Jamie said, splashing Rhi and me more furiously.

I'd had enough, what with Rhi's Monster Feet and now Jamie soaking me, there was no longer any point worrying what Daniel thought about me.

"Right, you've asked for it!" I cupped my hands and threw as much water at him as I could. "Get him, Rhi!" I yelled, and war was declared.

Five minutes later, the three of us were soaked through. Rhianna and Jamie continued the fight, laughing and yelling and chasing each other around like a couple of puppies. I waded out of the lake and threw myself down onto the ground next to Daniel. Jip lay by his side.

"I haven't even got a towel," I said with a lame laugh.

Daniel ignored me and continued staring out at the lake.

"Rhi's . . ." I wanted to explain my sister to him. I searched for the right words. "She's just kind of young for her age. She doesn't understand stuff."

"She's okay."

"Sometimes. Sometimes not."

"You can't choose your family—just your friends." He was scowling at Jamie.

"Jamie doesn't mean to be nasty, really he doesn't."

"Could have fooled me."

"He's just angry. That's all. Takes things out on other people."

There was a brief silence. Then Daniel looked at me sheepishly. "Me too."

We exchanged a small smile. The ice was broken.

I looked over the shimmering lake at two white swans dipping their black and orange beaks into the silky water, then turning their long graceful necks to preen their feathers.

"Pretty cool here, isn't it?" I said.

"They nested on the island last year," said Daniel quietly. "And the year before."

"Guess they know a good place when they see it . . . like your cave."

Daniel smiled. "Not very comfy, though—not exactly home, sweet home. . . ."

Now it was my turn to clam up. Daniel looked at me, his dark brown eyes becoming soft and gentle.

"Tell me what happened, Vicky."

I shuffled my feet, slightly embarrassed by his steady gaze.

"We were in foster care," I said. "Can't call that a proper home."

"S'pose not."

"Our mom's dead."

"Sorry."

"It's okay." I gave a little laugh to show him I was over it. "She died ages ago."

I tried to conjure up her face in my mind's eye, but it was as if some invisible force was rubbing out the details as fast as I tried to remember them. Shocked, I concentrated harder, but all I could see was the vague shape of someone wrapped in warm blankets and huddled in a deck chair.

"You all right?" Daniel asked.

"Course." I pasted on a grin. "So . . . is it fun having your parents teach you?"

He shrugged. "Not bad. Can't get away with the 'the dog's eaten my homework' excuse anymore, though."

I laughed a bit too loudly and a bit too long. Daniel looked at me. I needed to fill the gap, keep things normal.

"So aren't you s'posed to be, like, having lessons now?"

"Mom and Dad are redecorating, so I'm actually working hard on my project."

"What sort of project?"

"Astronomy."

"Wow. . . . I'm a Pisces, by the way."

"That's astrology."

"Only teasing."

"I'm Scorpio. Mean, moody and vicious when roused."

"Really?"

"No. I'm a wimp."

"You don't seem like a wimp. And I've met a few."

"Thanks. But take it from me, I'm wimp to the core."
There was a sudden edginess in his voice. Somewhere
along the line, the joke had disappeared and now he
sounded deadly serious. He seemed to realize and gave a
small laugh.

"Sorry. Told you I was mean and moody. So what
about your dad?"

The last thing I wanted to talk about was Dad, so I
started to trot out the old story about him being abroad.
Daniel was still looking at me, and I could feel my face
blushing beet red. I knew he didn't believe me.

"If my kids needed me, I'd be back like a shot," he
said quietly.

"Well, maybe our dad doesn't care about us," I said
with just a bit too much emotion in my voice.

"So you're running away from him too?"

There was an awkward silence. Daniel was watching
Rhi and Jamie in the lake. I felt the anger bubbling up in
me. Just who did this kid think he was?

"He's in prison, if you must know."

It felt good to blurt out those words. It was like a huge weight coming off me. Then, before I could stop myself, everything came tumbling out about Dad's depression and Mr. McCready's special deliveries.

Before I knew it, I was telling him how Dad got arrested. I'd never told anyone before. It happened a few weeks after we were taken into care. When he came to visit us, I'd noticed he looked more and more disheveled each time, like he'd given up or something. Then the visits stopped. A week later, Mrs. Frankish called to say that the police had stopped Dad on the highway. They said he'd been speeding and driving like crazy, swerving from lane to lane. When they looked in the van he was driving, they found it was full of stolen TVs. To cut a long story short, they arrested him, he went to court and was sent to prison.

Jamie and Rhi came running out of the water, and I clammed up again. Daniel didn't say anything, but he'd noticed I'd stopped talking. Those eyes didn't miss much.

"We're going to swim to the island," said Jamie. "You coming?"

"Jamie, be careful—"

"Vicky, don't be such a chicken. Just because you can't swim," Jamie taunted.

"I can . . . a bit." I looked at Daniel and could feel my face reddening again.

"I'll stay here with you," he said.

"Can't you swim either?" asked Rhi bluntly.

"Yeah, I can swim." I detected that cold note in Daniel's voice again. "I just don't want to, that's all."

"I bet you can't really," Jamie teased.

"Jamie!" I glanced at Daniel.

Daniel was glaring at Jamie. A hard glint came into his eyes. Mean, moody and vicious when roused.

"Bet you're scared like Vicky." Jamie started making chicken noises. "Bet you're just saying you can. That's what she does."

"Okay, I'll prove it." Daniel kicked off his sneakers. He pulled off his T-shirt and stood in front of us. I just managed to hide a gasp. Covering most of his chest and stomach was an ugly, dark purple blotch. The skin looked sore and angry.

"Come on, then," said Daniel, staring coldly at Jamie. "I'll race you to the island and back."

I looked at Jamie. He was fidgeting nervously, trying not to look at Daniel's torso but unable to stop himself. Rhi just stared unashamedly, her mouth open wide as Daniel turned and walked down to the water.

"It's okay," he snapped. "It's not contagious."

CHAPTER 27

Rhianna

Daniel was a much better swimmer than Jamie. He beat the pants off him. He beat me too, but only just. Vicky stood at the edge of the lake, but she didn't cheer us on. When we came out, Vicky made us dry ourselves with Jamie's sweatshirt. Then we all sat on the boat looking at the island and eating cheese rolls. I had three and I was still starving. Jamie didn't say anything. Nobody said anything. It was getting really boring all sitting around saying nothing, so I thought maybe I should say something.

"Daniel, what's that big purple splotch on your tummy?"

Vicky made a funny face and said, "Rhi . . ."

But I wanted to know. "Does it come off, like marker?"

"No."

"So what is it?"

"When I was nine, I tipped a saucepan of boiling water over me."

"Does it still hurt?" I asked.

"Only here." He pointed to his head. I didn't understand.

"Why?"

"Rhi, drop it." Vicky got up off the boat.

"Why, Daniel?"

"At school they called me Cootie Boy. One girl refused to swim in the school pool with me and got her parents to complain."

"You should have just whacked her one," said Jamie. Daniel ignored him.

"Is that why you don't go to school?" Vicky asked.

"What do you think?" He quickly pulled on his T-shirt, even though he was still wet. "We all run away from stuff we can't handle," he said, looking straight at Vicky, who went bright red.

"But what about your friends?" said Jamie.

"What friends? I was different. You know how it is. No one likes different." He got up. "And I was really stupid to think you guys wouldn't be the same."

I thought about my friend Maxine. There wasn't anyone like her.

"I like different," I said, picking up the last cheese roll and taking a big bite.

But Daniel wasn't listening. He'd already snatched up his sweatshirt and was marching off through the woods with Jip at his side.

CHAPTER 28

Vicky

We didn't stay long at the lake. Rhi kept asking why Daniel didn't like us anymore. Then the sun disappeared behind clouds and it got chilly. We started walking back through the woods in silence. Rhianna stuck close to me and jumped a mile every time she heard a sound.

"There's nothing to be scared of, Rhi."

"That's what you think," she replied, looking around nervously. We must have taken a wrong path because we found ourselves near the road. Jamie spotted something moving by the curb and wanted to go over to investigate.

"Better not," I said, turning back the way we came. "Someone might see us."

"Don't be a wimp, Vicky. There's no one around."
He ran off before I could stop him.

It was a rabbit. I thought it was dead at first because
it wasn't moving, but when we looked more closely, we
saw it was trembling slightly. Its eyes were wide open and
staring.

"Must have been hit by a car or something," said
Jamie. Rhi stroked the soft gray fur. The rabbit barely
flinched.

"Let's take it back to the cave and look after it," said
Rhi, gently picking it up.

I looked at the little bundle cradled in Rhi's big clumsy
hands and couldn't help thinking that things didn't look
very promising.

"Please, Vicky."

"I don't know. . . ."

Jamie scowled at me. "You wouldn't like to be left on
the road to be squashed, would you?"

Rhi joined in. "You wouldn't, Vicky."

I was definitely outnumbered. "All right." Suddenly I
was aware of a deep rumbling noise down the lane. And it
was growing louder. "Something's coming!" I hissed.

We dived for cover behind the hedge just as a school
bus turned the corner and pulled up ahead of us. The
door swished open and a shaven-headed boy of about

fourteen tumbled out, followed closely by a girl who yelled something rude at the driver as the door of the bus swished shut. The boy laughed, and the pair sauntered off down the lane, taking swipes at each other with their school bags, cheering when they scored a direct hit.

We waited till they were out of sight, then turned back into the woods.

"So much for not seeing anyone," I said.

There was a small village about a mile away from Great-Auntie Irene's house. This road must lead there, I thought. Dad and Great-Auntie Irene had walked us there once, but Mom had stayed at the house, too tired to join us. We'd gone to a little shop that had rows of glass jars full of all sorts of candy we'd never even heard of before. We were each allowed a little paper bagful—tangy cola cubes, chewy milk bottles, gummy bears and licorice that stained your mouth black. What I'd give for a bag of that candy now, I thought.

We found our way back to our cave. Jamie went straight in, took the old cookie tin down from the shelf and pulled it open. He lined it with his T-shirt before taking the rabbit gently from Rhi and placing it inside. He took his water bottle, poured a little over his finger and put it in front of the rabbit's mouth.

"Careful, Jamie. It might bite," I warned him. But the

rabbit didn't move. It just sat in the tin, staring straight ahead, helplessly.

"We can call him Peter," said Rhi. "Can I hold him again?"

Jamie passed the tin to her. She sat transfixed by the rabbit on her lap, hardly daring to move in case she frightened it.

I checked our supplies. We were down to some orange juice and a few potatoes.

"We could bake them in a campfire," said Jamie hopefully.

"We haven't got any matches."

"Who needs matches?" said Jamie, taking his camping book down from the shelf.

It was written by a man called Falcon B. Tremaine and had his picture on the back cover. He had a big fuzzy beard and wore a bush hat with a feather in the headband. He looked pretty tough except for the white socks he wore under his sandals. Jamie flicked through the pages until he got to the chapter about fire lighting. Concentrating hard, he slowly started reading. About ten minutes later, he looked up at us, his face like thunder.

"Stupid book!" he muttered, throwing it across the cave and stomping out, swearing under his breath.

"What's the matter?" asked Rhi.

I picked up the book and turned to the pages he'd been reading. There was a whole page on how to cut a square of turf from the ground and six detailed diagrams showing different ways of laying the twigs and kindling. I finally got to the crucial sentence.

"Strike the match close to the kindling and let it burn halfway down before applying it."

I quickly turned the pages looking for how to light a fire without matches. Nothing.

"We don't have any matches, you stupid fuzz ball!" I yelled at the photo on the back cover.

"I'm hungry, Vicky," Rhi said, stroking the rabbit. "And I want to see Daniel."

"Come on," I said. "Let's go and find him and try to make up."

Jamie didn't want to come at first, but he tagged along once Rhi and I set off. We made our way up the path to the end of Daniel's garden and saw him on the patio outside the back door brushing Jip's coat.

I exchanged grins with Rhi. He had his head down, and he hadn't seen us yet. We were just about to climb over the gate when the back door swung open. I pulled Rhi back, and we all hid behind the fence. His mom appeared and said something to him. He nodded, then gave Jip one last brush before disappearing inside.

"What do we do now?" asked Rhi.

I shrugged in reply.

But things were soon taken out of our hands. A few minutes later, the back door opened again and Daniel and both his mom and dad emerged. His dad was carrying a duffel bag, and Daniel had a backpack. His mom locked the back door.

"Are they going away?" asked Rhi.

"I don't know."

Daniel called to Jip, and they all disappeared around the side of the house. We heard the sounds of car doors slamming and then the starting of an engine.

We caught glimpses of the red car as it drove away up the lane. It was only then that the awful reality of our situation suddenly hit me. Daniel was our lifeline. Without his help, we were stuck.

CHAPTER 29

Rhianna

When we got back to the cave, Vicky said that there wasn't anything for dinner. Jamie wanted to eat the potatoes raw, but Vicky said raw potatoes were poisonous. Jamie didn't believe her, and when she wasn't looking, he took a big bite out of one. As he chewed it he made a face. Then he spat it out on the ground.

"Let's go to the shop and buy some stuff," said Jamie.

"Yeah, come on!"

But as usual Vicky was being a pain.

"No way. We can't risk it. They're looking for us. We all turn up at the shop, and that's it. Game over."

"We could dress up so no one knows it's us," I said.

"What as—the three little pigs?" said Jamie.

"Jamie's got his Spider-Man suit."

"Back home. And it's 'age five.' It doesn't fit anymore."

"Look, we're not dressing up, okay, Rhi? One, we've got nothing to dress up in, two, we'd look really stupid, and three, everyone would notice us."

"Forget it, Rhi," said Jamie. "We're not going to the shop."

"Well, I think it's a good plan."

"Trust me, it's not." Vicky went out of the cave, and Jamie turned to me.

"Come on. I've got an idea."

"What?"

"Let's go and find some roots and berries," he whispered.

"What for?"

"To eat, of course. That's what they always do in survival stories and stuff."

"Okay," I said.

"But don't tell Vicky."

"Why not?"

"Because she'll stop us. You know her."

"Yeah. Always fussing."

"Anyway . . . she wouldn't know a root if it was hanging off her nose," said Jamie with a giggle.

I gently put the tin down in a corner of the cave. I

tucked Jamie's T-shirt over Peter so he wouldn't be cold and put my little penguin next to him so he wouldn't be lonely, then we went out. Vicky was sitting outside. She asked where we were going.

"Nowhere," said Jamie.

"Don't go far."

"We won't."

"It'll be dark soon. Stay together!"

We followed the stream for a bit and then started looking for berries. I don't know where they all were, but we couldn't find any. We were just going to give up when I saw some green ones. Jamie thought they were blackberries that weren't yet ripe. There weren't any other berries, so I said to Jamie we'd better just get some nice roots. Jamie said good idea and started digging at the ground with his hands. They got covered in brown mud but he kept digging and digging one hole then another one and another. Then he pulled something up. It looked like a big hairy worm.

"I'm not eating worms, Jamie." Ollie Stanmore ate a worm once for a dare and then he was sick over Charlene Slackton's new shoes. They had peepholes, and it all squelched out over her toes. It made me feel yucky just thinking about it.

"It's not a worm, it's a root."

"Oh."

He put it to his nose and sniffed it.

"What does it smell like?" I asked.

Jamie shrugged and put it under my nose.

"Eurgh! Smells like a worm!"

"It's not a worm, all right? It's not a worm! It's a flipping root!"

I watched him sniff it again. He made a face then threw it back on the ground.

"Aren't you going to eat it?" I asked.

"No."

I was glad. Being sick was horrible. Especially when bits of chewed-up worm came out your nose.

"Let's just get some leaves instead," I said.

Jamie picked a couple off a tree, and we nibbled one each, but they were disgusting. We spat them out. It was getting dark, and Jamie was cross.

"If we could make a fire, we could have cooked a wild pig or something," he said.

"Where would we get a wild pig?" I asked.

"I don't know—here in the woods. . . ."

"But we can't even find any berries."

"Shut up, Rhi."

"I'm hungry!" I told him.

"So am I!"

"But you said we'd get something to eat. You said—"

"Shut up!" he shouted again.

"But—"

"Shut up, just shut up, or I'll . . . I'll cook your stupid rabbit."

I looked at him. "You wouldn't dare!"

"I would. Yum, yum. . . . Rabbit stew, here we come. . . ."

He laughed really nastily and turned around to go. I pushed past him and started running. I had to get back to the cave first to make sure he didn't touch Peter.

CHAPTER 30

Vicky

*I*t was getting dark when Jamie came back. I was furious.

"I said don't go far! Where on earth have you been? And where's Rhi?"

Jamie shrugged. "She ran off ahead of me. She should have been back ages before me."

"You let her go off by herself?"

He wouldn't look me in the eye. I caught hold of him, but he twisted away from me.

"I can't help it if she runs off, can I?" he shouted.

"Jamie—you know she doesn't go anywhere on her own. You know that. We have to look after her—she can't look after herself."

Jamie looked uncomfortable. I ran into the cave

and grabbed his flashlight from the shelf, glancing at the rabbit. It was still curled up in the tin next to the little penguin ornament. I could see its ribs faintly moving as it labored to breathe. I didn't need to be a vet to know things looked pretty hopeless.

Outside the cave, Jamie was scuffing the dirt with the toe of his sneaker. He looked upset.

"I'm going to find her," I said.

"I want to come with you."

"No. You've got to stay here. If she does find her way back, someone should be here."

I turned on the flashlight. A faint beam lit up a tiny circle of ground. Jamie made a face.

"The batteries are run down. I let Rhi play with it."

I quickly turned it off, thinking I might need it more later. I glanced around me. The woods looked different in the dimming light. Unfriendly and unwelcoming.

Then I thought of Rhi and I felt sick. I didn't like the dark much, but ever since Mom died, Rhi had been absolutely petrified of it. I had to find her quickly.

I scoured the woods, calling out her name. There was no reply, only the rustling of leaves and the scuffling of what I hoped were just cute little woodland animals. Once or twice I allowed myself to get spooked and swung around, terrified and convinced someone was following me. Then in the distance I heard the faint whine of motorbikes. Thinking I must be nearer the road than I realized, I turned away from the noise but must have misjudged where it was coming from, as the whine became louder and more insistent and grew into a roar. It was then I saw Jamie coming up behind me. The little tyke had followed me. I was furious and about to lay into him when, through the darkness, two separate headlights beamed around the woods, illuminating trees and bushes. I motioned to Jamie to hide, and we both ducked down low. Two dirt bikes threaded their way through the trees, revving as they mounted each slope and screeching noisily down the other side. I knew Jamie would have been impressed and just prayed that he had enough sense to keep his head down. We couldn't afford to be spotted by anyone. I watched the riders weave their way into the distance. At one point, one of them tried to swerve around a bush, but he misjudged the angle and nearly came off the bike, swearing noisily as he got his balance back and revved off. At last they were gone, the whining sound slowly faded and I got up from my hiding place. Without their headlights it was frighteningly dark. I called softly to Jamie and he emerged from the shadows. He was soaking wet.

"Couldn't you have found a dry place to hide?" I snapped angrily.

"I couldn't help it. . . . I slipped." He was shivering, and his teeth chattered uncontrollably.

"I told you to stay at the cave."

"I was worried about Rhi. It was my fault she ran off."

His grimy face was streaked with the tracks of his tears. I softened.

"Come on. We'll find her."

I turned on the flashlight. Its faint beam was pathetic, but it was all we had.

CHAPTER 31

Rhianna

It was too dark. And everything looked different. The cave wasn't where it was before, so I didn't know which way to go. I wanted Vicky, but I was too scared to shout for her in case they heard me. You know who I mean. The things with sharp teeth and claws, the things that come out from their hiding places just when you're on your own and suck out your insides before you even see them. The shadow things. I knew they were waiting. Hiding. They like the dark. They want you to think they're not there because you can't see them. But I knew just where they were. They were behind the trees. When the branches tap on your window in the middle of the night. That's them. I always asked the nurses to leave the light on in

Mom's room when she was in the hospital. Maybe one night they forgot so that was why she wasn't there in the morning. Maybe it was the shadow things that took her away.

I didn't want to think about this, so I kept walking really quietly. Then through the trees I saw some really bright lights moving about and it suddenly got noisy. It was people on motorbikes, but it was too late to run off. One of them shouted at me and pointed and then they both started riding their bikes around and around me in a circle like they were playing a game. I didn't like it. They didn't have helmets on, so I could see their faces. It was the boy and girl that got off the bus. They rode their bikes closer and closer. I was scared they were going to run me over.

I told them to go away, but they didn't listen. The girl looked at the boy, then turned around and, with a nasty smile, started to drive her bike straight at me. I shut my eyes and felt her whoosh past. The boy followed. The front of his bike scraped against my legs, and I fell over backward into the mud. They both laughed. I got up and ran. They chased after me for a bit, but then I tripped over a big sticking-out tree root and fell on the ground again. Now I started yelling and yelling as loud as I could. I didn't care anymore if the shadow monsters heard me or not.

CHAPTER 32

Vicky

We heard Rhianna's shouts and found her cowering in a ditch between some tree roots.

"Rhi! Are you okay?" I asked as Jamie pulled her to her feet.

"I told them to stop, but they wouldn't. They wouldn't stop!" She began crying uncontrollably.

I put my arms around her and hugged her tightly. Gradually the sobbing slowed, and we helped her brush the mud from her clothes and hair.

"It's all right now. They've gone. Let's get back to the cave. We'll be safe there."

We started to retrace our steps, but it was harder than I thought, and we seemed to be going in circles.

It was more by luck than judgment that we eventually found our way back. After seeing the same fallen tree for the second time, I was just beginning to give up when I spotted a stream. With our fingers crossed that it was ours, we started to follow it. Thankfully, it was our stream, and it led us all the way back to the cave. Jamie was quiet as he pulled off his wet clothes and crawled into his sleeping bag.

"I'm sorry, Vicky," he muttered as he snuggled down inside.

I heard a muffled sob from his direction and saw him turn his head away from me. I remembered he was only a kid.

"It's all right. Forget it now."

"But what are we going to do? We haven't got anything to eat. We've got to eat."

"Go to sleep now. Things'll look better in the morning."

I slept really badly that night. I had dream after dream about food. Plates of burgers and bangers and mash, piles of cakes and cookies—lovely, luscious, delicious food but always out of reach, either on the other side of a ravine or guarded by a pack of vicious wolves. I was just about to get my hands on a huge double-cheese pizza when I woke to find Rhianna shaking me. I looked out of the cave entrance and saw it was morning already. Jamie was awake too, and the pair of them were staring down at me as if I had the power to produce a full-blown fry-up breakfast from inside my sleeping bag.

"I'm starving. And so is Peter." She thrust the rabbit under my nose. Its eyes were glazed, and its nostrils caked with brown gunk. Food was probably the last thing on its mind. I looked at Rhi and Jamie, depending on me to do something. But what? I thought about Daniel. What if he had gone away for a few days? He and his parents had left carrying their bags. And they'd taken Jip. Even if Daniel was back now, he'd been really angry with us yesterday. What if he didn't want anything more to do with us? I sighed.

"Okay. I'll go to the shop. You can walk with me to town, but we're going to have to be very, very careful."

I reached over and found my purse. I emptied the contents onto my sleeping bag. My heart sank. We had precisely fifty-five pence. At least we could buy some matches so we could light a fire and cook the last few potatoes.

We reached the village just as the shop was opening up.

It was now or never. I turned to Jamie and Rhi.

"Wait here," I told them.

"But I want to come too," pleaded Rhi.

"No. You're supposed to stay here with Jamie."

"Please!"

"People are looking for three runaway kids. Our pictures have probably been on TV and in the papers. If I'm on my own, there's less chance I'll be recognized."

"But what if you get caught?"

I hesitated before I replied, hoping neither of them detected the worry hiding in my voice.

"I won't. Now stay out of sight. I'll be back in a minute."

I pulled the hood of my jacket over my hair, brushed a patch of dried mud off my jeans, then took a deep breath and started walking as calmly as I could toward the shop. I knew I had to behave as normally as possible but felt as if there was a hammer banging away in my chest that could be heard a mile away.

"Morning, dear."

"Hello." My voice wobbled. I pushed the corners of my mouth up into a smile as I tried to stop myself from shaking. I quickly walked past her and into the shop.

"Be with you in a moment," she called after me.

No one was in the shop. Near the door was a wire stand with fresh loaves of bread. The smallest loaf cost eighty pence. As I looked at it hungrily, my stomach gave out a huge rumble in sympathy. The delicious smell of fresh-baked bread filled the tiny room. I stared at the golden bumpy crust just waiting to be torn apart to reveal the soft white inside, and my mouth watered like it had never watered before.

Peeping through the door, I saw the woman with her back to me, chatting with someone. I reached out and tucked the loaf of bread under my arm. I knew what I was about to do was wrong but we needed food to survive. We were desperate. There were three sausage rolls on the rack underneath. I grabbed them too and stuffed them in my jacket pocket. Unable to stop myself, I wheeled around and filled my other pocket with several bars of chocolate. Then I shoved a bag of cookies inside my jacket, bracing my arm across my stomach to stop it from falling out. I was about to take a block of cheese when the woman bustled back in. I froze in panic, my face burning. I felt sick as I looked down at my scruffy clothes bulging with the things I'd stolen.

"Now then. Just the loaf was it, dear?" she asked.

She hadn't noticed the rest. I had to stay cool.

"Um . . . and a box of matches, please."

She turned momentarily to take down the matches from a high shelf. This was my chance. All I had to do was run past her out of the door and I'd be safe. For what seemed like an eternity but must have been only a nightmare split second, I hesitated, my feet rooted to the spot. The moment was lost as she swung around, blocking the shop doorway behind her. I was trapped.

"On holiday, are you, dear?" she said pleasantly as she handed me the matches.

I nodded dumbly, acutely aware of my bedraggled appearance and desperately praying she wouldn't notice my bulging pockets. The bag of cookies was threatening to slip out from under my jacket. I tried to edge it back up with my elbow.

The shop door opened. Someone else was coming in, but I didn't dare look. Another two seconds and my stash would come slipping out from under my jacket and cascade onto the floor. The police would be called, and we'd all be sent back in disgrace to Mrs. Frankish. This was it. The end of our journey. The end of us as a family.

"Lovely part of the world, isn't it? Wouldn't live anywhere else if you paid me," the woman was saying. "That's one pound and five pence, please."

Sweating and playing for time, I fumbled in my purse, then gave all the money I had to the woman.

"Ooh. There's only fifty-five pence here."

"Think you might have dropped this outside," said a voice from behind me. I swung around. It was Daniel.

He was holding out a fifty-pence piece. I had never been more glad to see anyone in my whole life.

"Oh, yes . . . thank you."

He handed it to the woman, and I didn't wait for her response. Red-faced with shame, I quickly scurried past them to the door and ran out across the road to where Jamie and Rhi were hiding. Daniel followed me out of the shop.

"What's up, Vick?" asked Jamie when he saw my face.

I shook my head. I couldn't speak. If I'd tried to say anything I knew I would have burst into tears there and then.

CHAPTER 33

Rhianna

I gave Daniel a big hug.

"We thought you'd gone away!" I said.

"I went over to my gran's for the night. We got home about half an hour ago."

"Come back with us to the cave, Daniel. I want to show you Peter."

"Who's Peter?"

"My rabbit."

I asked Vicky if it was all right if Daniel came with us. She didn't say anything. She just nodded.

"We can all be friends again," I told her.

She still didn't say anything.

"Don't you like Daniel anymore?" I asked her.

"It's not that," she said, kicking the ground.

"Didn't you get any food?" I asked.

"Yeah, I got some."

She wouldn't tell me what she got. She was in a moody. I don't know why. Jamie wasn't talking to Daniel either, so I walked with him and told him all about Peter.

Daniel said he'd show us a shortcut. As we walked past an old church, we saw two dirt bikes on the ground.

Then we saw them. They were sitting on the steps at the back, smoking and laughing.

"It's them from last night," I said, moving closer to Vicky.

Daniel was worried too. He looked around as if he wanted to run away. The girl looked up and stared straight at him.

"Hey, it's Cootie Boy!" she shouted. She threw her cigarette onto the grass. "How you doing, Cootie Boy?"

She laughed and turned to the boy. He nodded back at her. Then they got up and started walking over to us.

"Who are your saddo new friends, Cootie Boy?"

The girl stared at me. I tried to hide behind Vicky.

"Hey, it's that retard from last night—you want to

watch where you're going if you don't want to get run over . . . retard."

Jamie looked really angry—he was ready to whack them both. Vicky caught his arm and pulled him back.

"Let's just walk the other way," whispered Daniel, turning around.

"You're not running back to Mommy today, Cootie Boy. You stay right where you are!"

Daniel started to walk away.

"I said stay, Cootie Boy!"

Daniel stayed. He looked very small. The bullies went up to him.

"Now, then, what are you, Cootie Boy?" said the girl. "Tell these saddos what you are."

"He's our friend," I said to the girl. "Stop teasing him!"

"Stay out of this, retard," said the girl, spinning around to me.

Daniel stepped forward. "Leave her alone," he shouted in a wobbly voice. "She hasn't done anything."

"Ooooh. . . . Come over all brave, have we, now? That's new. I wonder what's got into Cootie Boy?"

"I'll find out," said the boy. He leapt on Daniel's back and locked his arms around his neck. Daniel struggled with him, but the boy was much bigger and stronger. Daniel started making coughing noises.

"Nope! Same old Cootie Boy!"

"Stop it!" Vicky shouted.

With a roar, Jamie ran forward, grabbed the boy and ripped him off Daniel. The boy yelled. He thumped onto the ground. Jamie dived onto him and sat on him so he couldn't get up. He was much smaller than the boy, but he was really, really angry now. When Jamie gets angry, you don't want to mess with him. Really, you don't. He pushed his face close up to the boy's. His caterpillar eyebrows were nearly touching him.

"Don't you ever pick on him or my sister or anyone, ever again!" said Jamie.

The boy started wriggling and kicking his legs around trying to get up. "Get him off!" he yelled. The girl grabbed at Jamie's hair and started pulling it.

Now Daniel tried to pull her off Jamie, but she punched him away like he was a little fly. Suddenly the boy kicked her right on the nose. I don't think he meant to do that. She let go of Jamie's hair. A trickle of red dribbled down onto her white shirt.

"You idiot! This is brand-new!" she screamed at the boy. She whacked him over the head.

"Wasn't my fault!" he whined. He rubbed his head with his dirty hand.

"Come on!" said Vicky. She grabbed my arm. We all started running.

"We'll get you back. . . . We will. . . . Just you wait!" the girl shouted.

CHAPTER 34

Vicky

We scrambled through the woods, along the stream and back to safety.

When we got back to the cave, Daniel turned to Jamie. "Thanks," he said quietly.

Jamie suppressed a grin. "Anytime," he muttered as he pretended to retie his shoelace.

Boys are such uncomplicated creatures; this was all that needed to be said.

Rhi grabbed the loaf of bread from under my arm. "Come on. I'm starving."

Daniel opened his backpack and took out a big plastic bottle of milk, a jar of peanut butter, a bunch of bananas and a huge bar of chocolate. "Bought it to go with the bread," he said with a smile.

I hurried into the cave and started unloading my stolen stash of food onto the shelf, too ashamed to tell the others what I'd done. I didn't hear Daniel come in and, turning around, dropped the handful of chocolate bars in surprise.

He looked at me, puzzled.

"Thought you didn't have any food—"

"I stole it all from the shop this morning," I mumbled, hanging my head and waiting for his reaction. "I'm a thief."

He didn't say anything for a moment. "Well, I guess you were only trying to look after Jamie and Rhi."

"But up till today I've never stolen anything in my whole life."

Suddenly I thought of Dad. How did he feel when he was delivering all those stolen TVs? Gramps, his dad, had been a policeman.

"Dad always used to tell us it was important to do the right thing. Not to tell lies. Not to cheat—even at Monopoly. Not to take cookies from the jar without asking. But then he goes and does a whopping great wrong thing himself. He knew full well it was wrong, but he carried on doing it again and again until he was caught."

"He must have been totally desperate," said Daniel. "Just like you were."

I felt the tears prickling in my eyes.

Daniel didn't say a word. He just wrapped his arms around me and hugged me. I felt calmer. I looked up at him.

"Thanks for what you did this morning. You were really brave," I said.

"You're joking, aren't you?"

"Not at all. First, in the shop you saved my skin, then when that horrible girl started on Rhianna . . ."

"I didn't do much, though, did I? If it hadn't been for Jamie—"

"Oh, Jamie's always fighting. It's like it's his hobby or something. You were really scared, but you still spoke up."

Daniel smiled at me.

"I couldn't sleep last night," he said. "I thought you were really angry with me for throwing a tantrum and leaving you at the lake yesterday. I thought I'd blown it and you wouldn't want anything more to do with me." He glanced at me, then added quickly, "You and Rhi and Jamie, I mean."

"Not a chance," I said, thinking how nice his eyes were when he smiled. "I . . . we all really like you."

Rhi came running into the cave. She saw Daniel's arms around me and did a double take.

"What's wrong?" she asked.

"Nothing," Daniel and I said at exactly the same time.

"Then why are you hugging?"

Daniel and I immediately stepped away from each other. I caught his eye, and we both smiled.

"Because we're all friends again," he said happily.

Breakfast was like a feast. A celebration. Maybe it was the food, or maybe it was just the fact we were all together, but everyone was in a good mood. Jamie and Rhi had made peanut butter, banana and chocolate sandwiches, and we washed them down with the cool fresh milk. Daniel wouldn't have any. He said he'd had a huge breakfast and happily watched as we demolished our meal. We joked and laughed about all sorts of silly stuff, like furnishing the cave with a few luxuries—maybe a DVD player and TV run off solar panels, a fancy barbecue to cook hot meals and a hot chocolate drink dispenser with marshmallows and whipped cream. We fantasized how we could happily live undiscovered at the cave for years. Finally, one day we'd come out of hiding like a bunch of Rip Van Winkles and surprise everyone with our reappearance.

When we'd finished every single crumb, we lolled back on the grass. Rhi carefully showed Daniel the tin containing the rabbit. He was hunched down even more on Jamie's T-shirt.

"I'm only keeping him till he's better," she told him, "then I'm going to let him free, because he's a wild rabbit, not a house one."

I watched as Daniel gently stroked the rabbit's back, then darted me a knowing glance.

"He's lovely and soft," he told Rhi.

It was late morning by now, and it was turning into another beautiful day. We decided to go down to the lake. Daniel said he'd come with us, and we made our way through the trees, laughing and joking.

We came to an abrupt halt as we reached the edge of the woods. Looking down toward the lake, Rhianna blurted out what I was just thinking.

"What if those bullies are down there waiting for us?" she asked fearfully.

"I'm not scared of them," Jamie replied with a scowl. But we still hid behind trees while he and Daniel checked out the shoreline. The place was deserted. Jamie beckoned to us, and we joined him and Daniel. The water looked deliciously cool and inviting.

"Hey, Daniel, you coming?" Jamie called as he waded in.

Daniel hesitated for a second. Then he quickly pulled

off his T-shirt, revealing the scars. This time Jamie didn't bat an eyelid.

"Bet you can't do handstands," he called.

"Bet I can!" Daniel replied with a grin, charging into the water.

I kept an eye on the woods, aware that someone might hear us or arrive at any second. Was this how it was going to be? I wondered. Always watching our backs to avoid being discovered? Running from place to place? Stealing? Hiding? What sort of future was that? The idea of living in our cave for as long as we wanted now seemed totally ridiculous. A little kid's fantasy, I thought flatly.

CHAPTER 35

Rhianna

Daniel showed me how to do handstands. They're easy peasy chocolate squeezy. You just dive under the water, plonk your hands on the squelchy weeds at the bottom and kick your legs up at the same time. But don't swallow any water. It tastes like mud. We practiced for ages. Vicky just sat on the grass with her arms hugging her knees.

"Vicky, watch me!"

I did my best handstand so far. She said it was really good, but she wasn't even looking.

"You didn't see it!"

"I did. . . . It was great." Her voice sounded funny, and she still didn't look up.

"Come in with us!" Jamie called, but she just shook her head. She looked very small scrunched up like that.

Daniel stopped and stared over at her. It was his turn, but he waded out and went and sat down next to her on the grass. I don't think she saw him because she still didn't look up. He put his arm around her. She didn't push him away, she just leaned on him and looked sad. I suppose she really wanted to do handstands like us. It's not very nice when you can't do things and everyone else can.

Jamie and I played for a while. Jamie wanted to do cartwheels, but they're really hard, so we did backflips instead. They're handstands but you go over and swoosh up through the water in a circle. We did thirty-seven each.

When we came out of the water, Daniel and Vicky were still sitting together talking.

"Don't be upset, Vicky. I can show you how to do handstands tomorrow—I'll hold your legs up for you."

"Thanks, Rhi," she said with a small smile.

Daniel grinned at her and then, do you know, she went all red and toothy just like she used to with Vomitty Matt.

Jamie didn't say anything. He was staring out over the lake. Suddenly he turned to us.

"Look!" he said, pointing at the road across the water.

Vicky went white, and Daniel jumped up like he had ants in his pants. I don't know what they were making such a fuss about. It was just two police cars driving along.

CHAPTER 36

Vicky

he cars are coming this way!" shouted Daniel.

"What are we going to do?" Jamie asked.

"They might not be after us. . . . It might just be a coincidence. . . ." But no one was listening to me, and a horrible feeling in the pit of my stomach told me that something was wrong. I remembered the woman in the shop—after I'd gone, she must have noticed stuff had been taken, put two and two together and realized who I was.

Daniel had taken Rhi's hand and had already started running.

"Back to the cave," he yelled. "It's your only chance!"

Jamie was hot on their heels. Quickly, I collected up our things and ran after them.

We reached the cave, panting and breathless. Rhi was crying, not sure what was going on. I took her inside and tried to calm her down while Jamie and Daniel worked furiously to remove any traces that betrayed our presence. Pretty soon, we heard voices.

"Jamie!" I hissed.

"Get inside!" called Daniel urgently to Jamie, then pulled brambles and wild roses over the mouth of the cave. "And don't make a sound! I'll head them off."

"I want Baby Emma!"

I peered out through the tangle of stems and leaves. Perched on a bush, Baby Emma and her wardrobe of clothes were sprawled in full view of anyone who passed.

The voices were getting louder.

"But I want Baby Emma!" wailed Rhi, her sobs becoming louder and more uncontrollable.

Jamie looked at me. He was thinking exactly what I was thinking. Springing into action, he pushed his way out of the cave, grabbed the doll and the clothes and sprinted back inside. Pulling the brambles back into place, he threw himself down onto the floor next to us, and we huddled together, hardly daring to breathe.

"Hey, you there!" a man's voice called out to Daniel. "Stay where you are, please."

We heard them scramble down the slope. There must

have been three or four of them. One of them slipped and swore noisily. The first man asked Daniel his name and address and if he'd seen any new kids around. Daniel kept his cool. He was amazing.

"There's always people around here. Holidaymakers and stuff."

"We're looking for three runaway children, two girls aged thirteen and a boy of ten. One of the girls was in the village shop this morning. Here're their photos."

There was a silence.

"Yeah . . . I saw her. She dropped some money, so I gave it back to her."

"Sergeant, take the others and have a quick look around. . . ."

I could feel the panic rising.

"She didn't hang about, though. She ran off toward Blakewell's Farm." I could hear the urgency in Daniel's voice as the policeman came nearer the cave.

"Blakewell's Farm, you say?" He was right outside the cave. Through the branches I could see his dark trousers and shiny black police boots splattered with specks of dirt and leaves. I had my arms around Rhi and didn't dare to breathe. I glanced over at Jamie. The whites of his eyes were wide and staring. He wasn't even daring to blink.

"Yeah . . . I'll show you where I saw her go, if you want."

"Okay, come on, then. Let's take a look." He called to his colleagues. "Hey—this kid saw one of the girls."

I breathed a sigh of relief. They were going.

"Oh, and another thing," the policeman said. "Their dad might show up. He's absconded from prison . . . probably looking for them."

My heart missed a beat. I glanced over at Jamie. Shocked and dazed as if someone had just hit him, he slowly turned and stared at me.

"It's all right," the policeman continued. "He's not dangerous, but we'd like him back behind bars."

The voices died away, but still none of us dared to move. After a few minutes, I slowly leaned forward to peep out. I felt my arm sharply pulled back as Jamie swung me around.

"You told us Dad was abroad, delivering stuff to refugees!"

He glared at me, his face buckling in anger and fury.

"I didn't want you knowing—"

"You didn't want us knowing where our own dad was?"

"Why's Dad in prison? What's he done?" asked Rhi.

"That stuff he used to deliver for Mr. McCready. It was all stolen."

"Was he a burglar?" asked Rhi.

"Course not. He was only trying to keep us all going!" shouted Jamie. "He wouldn't have done anything wrong if he didn't have to! He's our dad!"

Reddening, I remembered what happened in the shop.

"Jamie, I'm so sorry."

"We could have gone to see him in prison if we'd known! I hate you, Vicky Davies! You're so bossy . . . and you always think you're right!"

Jamie leapt up and barged past me out of the cave.

"Jamie . . . no! Where are you going?"

"Anywhere away from you!"

"Jamie, come back! You can't just run off like this!"

"Watch me!" he growled, jumping over the stream and disappearing into the woods.

CHAPTER 37
Rhianna

I want Jamie."

He'd been gone for ages. We sat on the cave floor. I had the tin with Peter in it on my lap. I wanted to go outside to get him some fresh grass, but Vicky wouldn't let me go anywhere.

"We've got to stay here, Rhi," she said.

"I want Jamie."

"He'll come back soon."

"When?"

She didn't say anything. Her eyes were red and puffy.

"When, Vicky?"

"I don't know. . . . When he's hungry. He always comes home when he's hungry. You know that."

"Let's go and look for him."

"We can't."

"Why?"

"Because there're police everywhere."

"But we could ask one of them to help us. Mrs. Edwards says if I get lost, I have to ask a police lady or a policeman or . . . um . . . just an ordinary lady on her own . . . or a lady with children . . . or two ladies together . . . or if I can't find any ladies on their own or with children or with another lady, then I have to ask a lady and a man, but—"

"Rhianna, shut up . . . please . . ."

"Nuckets to you."

I turned my back on Vicky. She hated that. I looked down at Peter. I touched his fur. He didn't move. I took him out of the tin and held him in my hands. His fur felt soft but his body was stiff.

"Wake up."

I poked him again really gently. He still didn't move. I showed him the penguin, but he wasn't interested. Vicky came over. She tried to put her arm around me, but I pushed it off.

"He was really ill, Rhi. . . . Too ill to live. He's dead now," Vicky told me.

"He's not. He's just asleep. You don't know anything.

Jamie was right. You think you know stuff, but you don't. He's just asleep because he's tired."

Vicky made a funny noise like she was going to start crying, then went and stood by the mouth of the cave.

I stroked Peter gently with just the tips of my fingers. When you're not well, you have to be looked after.

CHAPTER 38

Vicky

I left Rhi cradling the dead rabbit and crept out of the cave into the fresh air. I felt so sad for her and Jamie. I remembered those first few days after Mom died; Dad had shut himself away in his room, but Rhi hadn't been upset at all. I bit my lip as I realized she never really understood what it all meant, that it was final.

I wondered if the police had already found Jamie. I pictured him being driven back to the local police station, kicking the seat of the driver in front and trying to whack the policeman next to him. No wonder he was angry. He had a right to be. Jamie was only eight when Mrs. Frankish told us all Dad was going away and he wouldn't be able to take care of us or visit. Weaving a fairy tale about him delivering supplies for refugees was my idea. I know I should have told them the truth, but somehow it had just seemed so much easier to change the story.

Also, I couldn't bear the thought of anyone finding out—especially Jamie and Rhi, who both worshipped Dad. If Jamie had known, he would have immediately told his friend Sam, who would have told his mom and then it would have been around the whole town. Rosie would have heard and so would Matt and the evil Charlene Slackton. I'm sure Rosie would have been all right about it, although her parents might not have wanted her being friends with some prisoner's daughter.

As for Charlene Slackton—I could just imagine her blabbing nonstop to everyone. That girl had a mouth on her the size of a small country, and she wasn't afraid to open it and dish the dirt. Knowing her, we would have become the unfortunate spawn of an evil serial murderer. Exaggeration was her specialty.

Daniel didn't judge me when I told him where Dad was, but Matt probably would have run a mile. Vomitty Matt. What on earth did I ever see in him?

But I wasn't just trying to protect Jamie and Rhi and stop others from finding out. They weren't the only reasons I'd lied. It went deeper than that. Dad had left me on my own to look after Jamie and Rhianna. To be their mom and their dad. I was still angry with him for that.

I tried to push all thoughts of him out of my mind. It was his own fault, after all. He'd got himself into the mess he was in. And I didn't ask him to break out of jail and come after us. He didn't have to. He'd been in what they call a minimum-security prison, where the inmates sometimes went out to do supervised work. But he'd be in deep trouble when they finally caught up with him. So why had he risked everything to find us?

Then the simple truth hit me. He'd come after us because he still loved us and he still cared what happened to us. I felt a lump in my throat. I cared about Rhi, Jamie, and yes, even though I was still angry with him, Dad too. And the only thing that mattered right then was finding Jamie safe and sound.

I went back into the cave. "Rhi, come on. Let's go."

She insisted on bringing the dead rabbit. She put it gently back in the tin next to her little penguin and covered them both with Jamie's T-shirt so they wouldn't be cold. We crept out of the cave, searched the woods for a bit and then followed the stream down to the lake. We were about to give up when I looked out onto the island and saw someone half hidden behind a tree. Rhi saw him too.

"It's Jamie! Look, Vicky! He's on the island!"

Jamie must have heard us, as he looked over. Rhianna waved, but he didn't wave back. He quickly turned away and disappeared behind a bush.

I ran down to the old upturned dinghy, wondering what to do next. In the distance we heard the sound of dirt bikes. I scanned the woods and couldn't see them yet. But they were coming. Coming for us. Coming for revenge.

There was no way we could get back to the cave in time, besides which we couldn't leave Jamie on his own. I looked down at the boat. There was only one thing we could do.

"Quickly, Rhi. Help me!"

Together we turned the dinghy over and started to drag it down to the water's edge.

CHAPTER 39

Rhianna

"Rhi, climb in, hurry!"

I jumped in and sat on the wooden bench. I put the tin with Peter next to me. The roaring sound was getting louder. Vicky pushed the boat out and leapt in after me. Vicky took the oars and started to row across. She wasn't very good at it, and we went all zigzaggy. I looked down and saw there was water sloshing in the bottom of the boat.

"Use this, Rhi." She untied a small yellow bucket from the inside of the boat and gave it to me. "Scoop out the water and throw it over the side. As quick as you can."

I did what she said, but more water came in. So I scooped it out faster and faster, but it was no good. The water came up over my sneakers, wetting my socks and the bottoms of my jeans.

The bikers skidded to a halt when they saw us and started shouting and yelling. The girl was waving something. I stood up to get a better look.

"Sit down, Rhianna!"

"Leave my Baby Emma alone!" I shouted.

"Yee-ha!" yelled the girl, and she pulled off Baby Emma's legs and arms and head. She threw them all into the water.

They bobbed up and down for a bit, then they sank.

"Rhi, please, sit down—we'll tip over!" Vicky pulled me back down on the bench.

"Don't think you'll be hiding in your cozy little cave anymore!" shouted the girl nastily. She threw Baby Emma's body into the water.

The boy looked at the girl, and they grinned at each other.

"Yeah. Somebody seems to have trashed it!"

They both laughed.

"It's okay, Rhi. . . . It's going to be okay," said Vicky. "Don't cry."

I couldn't help it. I'd had Baby Emma right from when I was little. Mom bought her for me. She was my special doll.

Vicky kept her eyes on the island and tried to row faster. Suddenly, one of the oars popped out of its holder. Vicky caught it just in time, but she scraped her hand. It started bleeding. She just let the blood run down her arm and drip into the mucky water.

"Let Rhi row too!" shouted Jamie from the island. Vicky looked at me, then nodded. I stood to move next to her. The boat started rocking. It felt really wobbly, and I didn't like it. I nearly fell backward, but I got onto the bench and Vicky gave me one of the oars. It was better with two of us. It was like a race but with people swearing at us instead of cheering us on. Vicky was breathing really fast. We were nearly there, but the back of the boat was sinking lower and lower in the water.

At last the bottom of the boat scratched on the ground. We jumped out. The water came up to our knees. It was cold and muddy. Jamie rushed up to us and helped pull the boat onto the grass.

"We know who you are," yelled the boy. "Saw your ugly faces on TV."

"Three stupid little runaways," shouted the girl.

"What are we going to do, Vicky?" I asked. "I'm scared."

"They can't get us out here."

"They better not!" said Jamie.

I wanted to go around the other side of the island so the bullies couldn't see us, but Jamie said we should keep an eye on them. So we sat down and waited. And waited. Vicky thought they might just go away if we waited long enough. They finally stopped shouting and sat on their bikes, staring at us.

I looked down at Peter. I was glad I hadn't left him in the cave. They might have hurt him too. He still hadn't moved. Then I had a horrible thought. Maybe Vicky was right. Maybe he was already dead.

I asked Jamie. He was watching the bullies in case they tried to swim over to us. He looked at Peter and nodded.

"Sorry, Rhi."

I thought hard for a moment.

"Mom's dead . . . but she's coming back one day, isn't she?"

Jamie looked at Vicky, then back at the bullies.

"She can't, Rhi," said Vicky really quietly.

"Never? Not even for a day or something?"

"No."

"Not even for . . . five minutes?"

"No."

"One minute?"

"No."

"What about just to say hello then go again?"

"Rhi, she's not coming back, all right? Never. Not at all!" said Jamie in his "shut up or I'll whack you" voice.

"But that's not fair!" I felt cross now. Nobody had told me that before. "So where's she gone?"

Vicky and Jamie were staring at the bullies. They wouldn't even look at me. Vicky's mouth was all twisted up.

"Where is she?" I asked.

"Dunno. Heaven or something," said Jamie.

"So where's that, then?"

"Don't know. . . ."

"Vicky?"

She shrugged. "Up in the sky somewhere. . . ."

"How can you live up in the sky?" I said.

Jamie and Vicky went quiet. They didn't even know. I looked over at the bullies sitting on their bikes.

"I wish she was still here, not up in the sky, jumping around on clouds." I had another thought. "So why hasn't Peter floated up to the sky, then?"

Vicky gave a big sigh. "Look, Rhi. The bodies die. They don't work anymore."

"But you said—"

Jamie was getting cross. "Shut up, Rhi."

"I'm only asking."

"Well, don't ask. Not now. Just shut up."

"But I want to know. Mrs. Edwards says we should ask a question if we don't understand."

Vicky looked at Jamie, then said quietly, "Okay, so maybe it's just their spirit that stays alive."

"What's that?"

"It's what's inside them. It's invisible, but it makes them who they are—it makes them different from anybody else."

I thought hard for a bit, then I stroked Peter for one last time. I put him back in the tin and tucked Jamie's T-shirt over him. I took out my little penguin and zipped him safely in my pocket. I fixed the lid on the tin really gently, then I put the tin down between two tree roots and covered it with moss and leaves. Vicky was watching me.

"What are you doing?" she asked.

"I don't think Mom's spirit is floating around in the sky. I think it's here because this is her favorite place that she liked more than anywhere else. She told me. I'm leaving Peter here so they can be together."

CHAPTER 40

Vicky

*I*t'll be all right, Vicky," said Rhi. "Don't worry."

A huge lump rose up in my throat. It was the first time in our whole lives that Rhi had ever comforted me. I thought about Mom. What would she do if her spirit was here with us? What would she say? I concentrated hard but felt nothing.

Rhianna's wrong, I thought flatly. You aren't here, Mom, are you? We're on our own. I looked across the lake. There was a wind now, and small waves formed, making the water choppy and dark. Thick gray clouds were rolling over, covering the blue sky like a dull, heavy blanket.

The beady-eyed girl was busy talking into her cell

phone. When she'd finished, the shaven-headed boy ran down to the water's edge and shouted over to us.

"Hey, saddos! Guess what? The police were really interested to know where you are. Looks like you'll all be going home!"

"Let's get out of here," said Jamie, looking at the boat.

"But the bullies'll get us!" wailed Rhi.

"We can't, Jamie," I said. "There's a leak. We'll never make it . . . and I can't swim."

"I'm not waiting for the police to turn up."

He searched for the hole in the bottom of the boat.

"It's not that big," he said, ripping a bit of his T-shirt, then using the cloth to plug the hole. "We'll be all right. It's our only chance."

I looked at the old, battered dinghy. I wasn't happy, but Jamie was already pulling it back to the water's edge and calling to us to jump in. The beady-eyed girl started yelling.

"Hey! Where d'you think you're going?"

"Yeah—you can run, but you can't hide! They're going to get you," called the boy. They both laughed.

I took a deep breath. We had no other choice. We climbed into the boat, and I prayed that it would be all right.

"It's not far, Vicky," Jamie said, noticing my petrified expression. Taking up the oars, he started to row steadily.

There was still some water coming in, and Rhi and I took turns bailing it out. But as fast as we bailed, more water flooded in. The cloth plug had come loose and was floating around the bottom of the boat. I grabbed it and tried to put it back, but I couldn't find the hole.

"Jamie . . ."

"We're nearly there."

He was trying to keep calm, but I could hear the note of panic rising in his voice.

On the shore I saw Daniel run out from the woods and up to the lake edge. Ignoring the jeers and catcalls from the two bullies, he started waving and calling to us.

"Daniel!" I yelled. "We're sinking!"

The back of the boat was submerging faster now. With a sudden *whoosh*, water came flooding in over the rim and the boat dipped below the surface. For a split second, we were sitting in water up to our waists.

The boat wobbled.

"Quick, jump out!" shouted Jamie. "We'll have to swim for it!"

Jamie and Rhi leapt out of the boat, but I sat there frozen, unable to move as the boat sank.

I screamed as I felt nothing but the dark inky water

beneath me. It was deep down there. Very deep. Panicking, I thrashed my arms and legs as my head went under and I got a mouthful of dirty water. I coughed and spluttered, fighting my way up to the surface to gasp a breathful of air.

I called for help, but I could feel myself going under again. There was nothing I could do. I was being sucked down into the lake's depths, into its calm silence. An icy numbness spread through my body, and it was then that I realized I was going to die.

I was sinking farther and farther down, lightly, delicately, weightlessly. Within the still quietness I heard a small, familiar voice in my head. It was Mom's. She was telling me I would be okay. But how do you know, I thought. How do you know? You're not with me—you're gone.

Then a vision of Mom flashed before me. She looked beautiful, exactly like she did before she got sick. A bright light glowed behind her. Her thick golden brown hair shone as it fluttered around her face. She looked straight at me. I could see the freckles over her nose and even the tiny pink scar on her jaw. She smiled and her lips parted showing her teeth, straight and white and even. I felt completely and absolutely happy. Nothing mattered anymore as long as I could stay with her forever.

I reached out my hand to touch her, but suddenly

from behind, someone grabbed me and started pulling me up and out from under the murky blackness, away from Mom and the light. I watched, powerless, as, still smiling but becoming fainter and more distant, Mom slowly raised her hand and waved good-bye to me.

We burst through the surface of the water, spluttering and gasping for air.

"It's all right, Vicky. . . . I've got you," I heard a voice say. It took me a few moments to realize it was Rhi. I tried to speak, but the effort was too much. I clung limply on to her as she dragged me awkwardly through the water toward the shore.

Daniel and Jamie swam up to us. They both looked terrified. I wanted to tell them I was okay, but just turning my eyes toward them was all I could manage.

Somehow or other, we made it to the shore. Daniel and Rhi half carried, half dragged me onto the grass and turned me on my side. In one huge, choking splutter, I brought up gallons of lake water and then gasped in a huge breath of air.

I looked at Rhi anxiously standing above me, dripping with water. Mom had told me everything would be all right.

I forced out a whisper. "Thanks, Sis."

Rhi bent down and hugged me tight. I closed my eyes, exhausted with the effort. Daniel marched over to the bullies and told them to get lost. The beady-eyed girl looked like she was going to give him a mouthful, but there was something in his voice, a different, new note. Something that said "don't argue." The pair got back on their bikes and revved off into the woods.

I couldn't stop shivering. Daniel picked up his nearby sweatshirt and put it over me. He sat down next to me as I lay helpless on the grass and waited. Slowly, minute by minute, I began to feel better. My breath came more easily and evenly. Gradually I stopped shaking.

I looked up at Daniel and gave him a small sad smile.

"I'm going to really miss you," he said quietly.

"Not as much as I'll miss you," I replied, impulsively reaching for his hand and giving it a gentle squeeze. Daniel looked straight at me with those big soft brown eyes, then suddenly leaned over and kissed me long and tenderly on the lips. He sat back and looked at me again, but for once I knew I wasn't blushing.

"Sorry," he mumbled.

"Don't be," I heard myself saying. "I've been wanting you to do that for ages."

We heard them coming with their sirens wailing

and their blue lights flashing, but there was no dramatic capture. No big scene. We were all taken wet and bedraggled and wrapped in blankets to get checked out at the local hospital. Rhi was crying softly as we drove away, but I knew deep inside it wasn't over.

CHAPTER 41

Rhianna

Daniel's mom came to get him from the hospital, but we had to stay there all night. They put Vicky in a room on her own, but Jamie and I were in the big ward with lots of other children. It was really noisy and busy and hot, and I couldn't get to sleep, even though I put my little penguin on my pillow next to me. The nurses kept going into Vicky's room, but when I asked if she was all right, they just said she was doing fine.

The next morning Vicky was still asleep and Jamie and I were having our breakfast when one of the nurses came over.

"You've got a special visitor," she told us. "We don't usually let anyone on the ward this early—but we've made an exception."

I thought it was Daniel, but then a policeman came in with another man.

"Dad!" Jamie yelled.

I wasn't so sure. This man didn't look like our dad at all. This man looked worn out. He had a beard and his hair was long and his clothes were scruffy. And he was wearing a metal bracelet, which was joined to the policeman.

"Is it really Dad?" I whispered to Jamie.

Jamie leapt up and threw his arms around him.

"Course it's Dad!"

I jumped up too, and we both hugged him together.

"Am I glad to see you two!" Dad said, hugging us back tightly with the arm that didn't have the bracelet.

"Are you in trouble?" Jamie asked, looking at the policeman who was standing next to Dad.

Dad made a face. "Just a bit."

"Did you run away too?" I asked.

He nodded. "I was frantic. Couldn't think of anything else but finding you all. I was racking my brains trying to figure out where you might be, then yesterday I woke up with this weird feeling you were at Great-Auntie Irene's.

I hitched a ride." He looked down at the floor. "I didn't know she'd died," he said quietly. "I hid in the woods all day, wondering what to do next. That's where they picked me up, yesterday evening."

"What was it like in prison?" I asked.

Dad started telling us about it. It sounded a bit like some of the children's homes but bigger and for grown-ups. Dad had worked in the prison gardens, and now he knew about growing all kinds of stuff—tomatoes, beans, cabbages, potatoes, carrots, peas and loads of other things. Sometimes they let him out to work on a farm, and that's how he escaped. He was supposed to be picking lettuces, but he crept out of the greenhouse when no one was looking.

I told him about the stinky children's homes and Sarah and Paul and the baby. He went all quiet when he heard how we were going to be split up.

He told us he was sorry for what he'd done, he had been stupid and if there was any way he could make it up to us, he would. He said life was going to be better from now on. He wasn't ever going to be a truck driver again because he wanted to be home more, and he was never, ever going to do anything wrong like delivering McCready's stolen goods.

"You're going to take care of us when you get out of prison, aren't you?" Jamie asked.

Dad looked down at the floor again.

"Dad? You'll take care of us, won't you?" I said.

He looked at the policeman standing next to him. "I want to . . . if they'll let me," he said quietly.

CHAPTER 42

Vicky

"Vicky..."

I knew that voice. My head was thumping, but I forced myself to try to place who it was. I couldn't understand why there were so many people around my bed—Rhi, Jamie and two men. I was afraid for a second, not sure where I was.

"It's Dad, Vicky," came Rhi's voice.

"Dad?"

Puzzled, I lifted my head and looked at the men again—there was a policeman in uniform and handcuffed to him was . . . Dad. He looked a mess. I glanced at the shiny handcuffs as he shifted from foot to foot, trying to hide his wrist behind his back.

"Dad . . ."

He looked at me uncertainly.

I reached out my arms. His face lit up, and he lurched forward, almost jolting the policeman off his feet.

"I'm sorry, Vicky," he whispered gruffly. "I'm so sorry. I've missed you all so much."

As hard as I fought them back, I could feel hot tears welling up in my eyes. Dad was crying too.

"I've missed you too, Dad."

All the anger that had been stored up in me for the last two years suddenly ebbed away like the tide on a beach. When Mom died, Dad's world had fallen apart too. He'd been just like me, trying to get through all the bad stuff as best he could, making bucket loads of mistakes along the way.

CHAPTER 43

Rhianna

Mrs. Frankish came to the hospital in the afternoon and told us off five times for running away. I counted. She was really angry and said we'd generated mountains of paperwork for her to handle. Jamie asked how she got into her office if there was a mountain inside, but she didn't say. She was too busy complaining.

When the doctor said we could go home, I was waiting for Dad to pick us up, but he never came. I kept telling Mrs. Frankish I wanted to go home with him, but she said we'd be lucky if that happened. She told me it was going to take a while before he was allowed out of prison, and besides that, he was in a lot of trouble for running away.

I wanted to go and stay with Elizabeth again, but Mrs. Frankish said we couldn't and told us that just for the weekend we were going to stay with a couple who lived nearby. She said they fostered kids in an emergency. Their house smelled of fried onions, but it was nice and quiet, and the next day Vicky didn't wake up till teatime. They had a big white cat called Egbert. He let me stroke him under his chin.

On Monday morning Mrs. Frankish picked us up in her car. She said we were going to go to a group home near where we used to live with Sarah and Paul. It took us ages to get there, and Jamie got sick because he ate a whole bag of Jelly Babies. We had to have the windows open for the rest of the way.

We only stayed there for a few days because two of the kids were away and we had their rooms. I didn't mind because it was a horrible place anyway, but Vicky was getting really fed up. Then Mrs. Frankish told us she'd managed to find a lady called Sandy who could foster us for a few weeks. Vicky got mad and asked what was going to happen after that, but Mrs. Frankish just said there'd be a meeting to decide.

So we went to Sandy's next. She lived in a little house at the end of a long row of little houses. She didn't have a front yard—you just went straight in from the sidewalk.

Mrs. Frankish rang the bell, and a big fat lady in a swirly-colored dress opened the door.

"Come on in," she said. "I'm Sandy."

Mrs. Frankish said good-bye, and we went inside and followed Sandy down a long, narrow hallway. On the walls were rows and rows of photos of kids.

"Are these all your children?" I asked.

"Foster children," she said with a smile.

"But where do they all sleep?" I said. I had peeped into her tiny living room. How would they all squeeze in to watch TV?

"Oh, they don't live here now." Sandy laughed. "I've been fostering children for a long time. Over thirty years. Most of these are grown up. Some even have children of their own."

We went into the kitchen. It was a bit of a mess. There were bowls and spoons and packets of sugar and flour and some eggshells and on a wire rack by the oven a heap of lovely-smelling cupcakes.

"Had a spare half hour before you arrived," Sandy said. "You do like cupcakes, don't you?"

Jamie grinned. "Nah. . . . Hate them."

Sandy laughed and made a sad face. "Oh, darn. There goes my diet again. . . ."

"I'll eat them for you," I told her.

"Thanks, Rhianna," said Sandy. "You can help me ice them first, if you like."

The cupcakes were yummy, and we had three each.

We went back to our last school the next day. It was nice to see Maxine again. Her mom had braided her hair with beads, and she looked really pretty. I showed her the little penguin Elizabeth gave me and let her stroke it for luck. It worked because Mrs. Edwards let us do clay all afternoon. We rolled out long snakes, then wound them around and around to make little pots.

Charlene Slackton's going out with Vomitty Matt now. Vicky said they deserved each other. She doesn't like him anymore—she likes Daniel now. She talked to him for hours and hours on Sandy's phone last night.

After Vicky put down the phone it rang again, and she said she'd answer it because it was probably Daniel calling her back, but it wasn't. It was Mrs. Frankish. She said the special meeting would be tomorrow at her office.

She told Vicky there would be some very important people there and we all had to be on our very best behavior. I'd rather go to McDonald's.

Vicky asked her if we were going home with Dad after the special meeting, and Mrs. Frankish told her the issues were very complex. She always uses words like that. I think she makes them up so we can't understand what she's talking about. I asked Vicky what Mrs. Frankish meant, but she just got cross and told me not to get my hopes up. Jamie said not to worry. If they didn't let Dad take care of us, he'd whack them all in their rudey bits, and he didn't care if they were very important people. Vicky didn't even bother telling Jamie off.

She was really moody all evening, and she started biting her nails again. She chewed them right down to the pink skin, and she even made her little finger bleed.

CHAPTER 44

Vicky

*T*hat night was the longest I'd ever known. Sandy said we ought to get a good night's sleep to be ready for the meeting the next day, so we all went up to bed at nine. Rhi fell asleep quite quickly, convinced that tomorrow she'd be back with Dad, but I lay in bed listening to the sounds of the night, unable to relax.

Niggling worries kept burrowing their way into my mind, churning up my thoughts and pulling them one way, then another. By running away, Dad had got himself in deep trouble. But had he also blown his chances of taking care of us when he got out of prison? I just didn't know. Social workers were supposed to keep families together, weren't they? But I didn't think I'd ever heard Mrs. Frankish say one good word about him.

I turned over, trying to blank out the bad thoughts and concentrate on the good. Us being together again. It wasn't so much to ask, was it? It wasn't as if we were asking for the moon!

I must have slept because I was woken up by Rhi's voice calling my name. I opened my eyes and saw her staring down at me.

"Vicky! Come on. Wake up! Sandy says we've got to get ready. We're going soon!" She turned back to her bed and, taking her little penguin from her pillow, stuffed it into her pocket for luck.

Sandy took us by bus to the offices where Mrs. Frankish was based. Rhi talked excitedly to Sandy the whole way about how we were all going to live with Dad and grow veggies and how she'd have a pet rabbit or ten. I glanced at Jamie. He was sitting completely still, his eyebrows knitted together in an angry scowl. He'd hardly said a thing all morning.

The bus lurched to a halt, and we climbed the steps to an official-looking glass-fronted building. I gulped in some air. This was it. The place where our future would be decided.

Inside, the receptionist directed us to a waiting room where a serious-looking man in a gray suit finally came in and told us to follow him. Sandy flashed us a small hopeful smile and wished us luck, and then we were whisked away.

CHAPTER 45

Rhianna

The man took us into Mrs. Frankish's office. It was cold and smelled like mushrooms. It had stripy paper on the walls and a big whiteboard you could draw pictures on, but nobody had. There were shelves from the ceiling to the floor, and they were full of books and folders and piles of papers. Mrs. Frankish sat behind a desk. She was wearing a black suit with silver buttons. It had long sleeves and a high neck that looked like it might choke her. She didn't smile at us, not even once. She told us to sit down and pointed to some chairs with her bony hand.

Sitting next to her was a man with glasses and long gray hair in a ponytail and a woman with big sticking-out teeth who smiled at us all the time.

The man was looking through some papers on his lap.

"Where's Dad?" I asked.

The man looked up and stared at me over the top of his glasses. The smiley woman with the teeth turned and whispered to Mrs. Frankish, who whispered something back.

"Your father isn't coming today, Rhianna," the woman said very slowly and very loudly with an even bigger smile.

"You don't have to talk to her like she's stupid," growled Jamie.

The woman with the teeth put them back in her mouth. Vicky told Jamie to shush, so Jamie gave her a shove and nearly pushed her over.

"Jamie has a few anger management issues," Mrs. Frankish said, and the man with the ponytail nodded, but the woman with the teeth wasn't smiling anymore.

"This meeting is merely for myself and my colleagues to assess where you'll be best placed in the future," said Mrs. Frankish.

The woman with the teeth said they'd better begin as she had another very important meeting in half an hour.

The ponytail man started asking us loads of questions about where we went and what we did when we ran away. Vicky did most of the talking, except when Jamie butted in and said something rude. Then they asked me what it was like after Mom died when Dad was looking after us.

"It was great," I said.

"In what way was it great?" asked the ponytail man, looking at me over the top of his glasses.

I thought for a bit.

"We had jam sandwiches every night for dinner. Or ramen noodles. And we didn't have to have baths or brush our teeth or hair."

Vicky started to say something, but the man stopped her and said he wanted to hear from me.

"Go on," he said.

"And we stayed up really late."

"Did your father allow that?"

I nodded. "He didn't mind."

"And why do you think he didn't mind?"

"Because he told me nothing mattered anymore."

Mrs. Frankish whispered something to the ponytail man. The other lady was busy writing things down. I started telling them about the day the men took all the furniture away and how it was fun sleeping on the carpet instead of beds, but I don't think they were really listening.

Mrs. Frankish put up her hand and said, "Thank you, Rhianna. You've been very helpful."

She looked at the other two, then said, "I don't expect we'll need long to come to our decision."

The ponytail man nodded. The lady with the teeth smiled her big smile again.

"So if you children will just go down to the waiting room for a short while—"

"Because I was helpful, does it mean we're allowed to live with Dad?" I asked Mrs. Frankish. She was shuffling the papers on her desk.

"Tell Sandy we'll only be a few minutes," she said.

Jamie stood up and kicked over his chair. "We're not going anywhere until you tell us we can live with our dad."

"Pick that up on your way out, please, Jamie," said Mrs. Frankish.

Vicky stepped forward. "Jamie's right," she said in a wobbly voice. "We're not leaving."

"And what's more, I'll whack you all if you say we can't!"

"Yeah," I shouted. "And if you make us live somewhere else, we'll just run away again!" I turned to Vicky. "We *will* run away, won't we, Vick?"

CHAPTER 46
Vicky

I looked at Jamie and Rhi's furious and expectant faces and slowly shook my head.

"No. We're not running away again."

"Vicky!" Jamie and Rhi howled at me, their eyes wide in disbelief.

"But we want to live with Dad!" said Rhianna.

"Running away again isn't going to make that happen, Rhi," I said quietly. "It's not going to solve anything."

The toothy woman looked at her watch. "I'm afraid I really do have another meeting, so if you could just leave us to our discussion—"

"Please . . . wait," I pleaded helplessly. "These are our lives you're deciding on."

She glanced at Mrs. Frankish, unsure whether to ignore me or not.

"We will choose the option which is in all your best interests," said Mrs. Frankish firmly. "Now, if you could go down to the waiting room for a few minutes, we'll make our decision."

The ponytail man and the toothy woman both nodded in solemn agreement.

"You're going to split us up, aren't you?" My voice sounded odd, as if it didn't belong to me.

"We will have to consider all the relevant factors," said the ponytail man.

"But you don't even know our dad," I blurted out.

"We've heard what happened after your mother died."

"But that's just it," I said, standing up, my face burning red. "Our mom *died*. She was very sick and she died and it was sad and horrible. But it wasn't just awful for us—Dad was heartbroken too. He was so messed up, he just couldn't cope with taking care of us at the same time."

Mrs. Frankish frowned. "We know that, Vicky, but—"

"But that's the whole point," I interrupted. "You only know about Dad *after* Mom died, but you don't know anything about him before she died—you don't know what sort of dad he really is at all."

There was a silence. As I searched their faces for some kind of positive reaction, I could feel my heart thumping against my ribs as if it might explode at any moment.

"Tell us, then," said Mrs. Frankish gently, after a moment or two. "Tell us what your dad was like before your mom died."

Suddenly all those special memories that I had deliberately suppressed over the last couple of years came flashing back.

I could picture us all about four years ago in the garden of some stately home we visited and hear our excited squealing laughter as we followed Dad, stretched out and rolling over and over down a grassy slope to Mom, who was laughing at the bottom.

Back home in our little kitchen, I could smell Dad's delicious tomato sauce bubbling on the stove while we watched him fork out a long skein of spaghetti from another pot and wobble it about pretending it was alive so he couldn't nibble the end to check that it was done.

Out in our street I could see myself, much younger still, on my little pink bike—I could feel the exhilaration spreading through me as Dad let go of my bike and chased beside me on the sidewalk, shouting, "Keep going, Vicky! Keep going!" knowing all the while he was there in case I fell.

And then one of my earliest memories. . . . I was on our stairs in the dark, I could smell the pine scent from the Christmas tree as I wandered down crying from a bad dream and found Dad and Mom laughing together as they wrapped up presents in the living room. I could feel my cheek against the soft bumpy wool of his blue sweater as he carried me back up to bed, whispering softly that everything was all right.

I felt a surge of happiness. But where should I begin? How could I explain our wonderful, funny, kind dad in just a few sentences? I looked at Rhi and Jamie—their expressions were serious. The toothy woman glanced at her watch and fidgeted, and immediately I knew exactly how to start.

"The most important thing to know about our dad is that he always made time for us. He used to work really hard, but when he got home, it didn't matter if he was tired or busy or had tons of other things to do, he'd always find the time to listen to us, or talk about stuff or just play."

"It's true," interrupted Jamie. "Every Saturday he'd take us to the park and play football or whatever we wanted."

"And at bedtime he'd read us each a story," Rhi added. "I always wanted the same one. It's called 'We're

Going on a Bear Hunt.' It's really good. It's all about catching a bear."

Another memory bounced into my head.

"Hey, remember when Jamie left the door to his hamster cage wide open?" I asked Jamie and Rhi, who immediately grinned and nodded.

"Jamie came downstairs yelling that Mr. Spud had escaped," I continued. "He was so upset. We looked everywhere, turned the house upside down. . . . Then Mom thought she heard a scratching noise in the bathroom. Dad checked and saw a little hole in the corner, so he peeled back the linoleum and spent the whole evening taking up all the floorboards. And then finally he said he thought he could see Mr. Spud, so Jamie got the cage ready and Dad stretched his arm down and under and felt around and brought out one of Rhi's old socks! Then the nesting stuff in the cage wobbled and Mr. Spud popped his head out and looked at us all as if to say, 'Keep the noise down, will you?' He'd been there all the time, fast asleep.

"And Dad looked at Mom and all the floorboards and all the mess, and we thought he was going to explode, but he didn't. . . . He just said, 'Well, that's sorted out, then. Sorry to disturb you, Mr. Spud,' and laughed. He was so patient . . . even when we were naughty."

"When I was little, I took all the eggs out of the fridge and dropped them in his boots," said Rhi.

"I made an insect zoo in his lunch box once." Jamie giggled. "Dad said he jumped a mile when he opened it because a load of beetles flew out in his face. But when he got home, he didn't shout at me or anything."

"I can only remember one time when I saw him really angry. And it wasn't with us," I said. "Rhi and I were signed up for swimming lessons, but they wouldn't let Rhi join the class. Health and safety, or some stupid excuse. Dad was furious, and he went up to school to see the swimming teacher. When he came back, he didn't say much, but that evening he picked up Rhi's swimsuit and towel and told her they were going down to the swimming pool. He took her every Monday and Thursday evening for a year and taught her to swim himself. When they had a meet at school in the summer, he made sure she was entered for it—"

"And I won three races!"

There was a loud knock on the door. It swung open, and the man in the gray suit popped his head in.

"Mrs. Trevellian—they're all waiting for you."

The toothy woman darted him a vague look. "I'll be with you in a moment," she said.

The man nodded and went.

Mrs. Frankish looked at her watch, then turned to us.

"I think you three had better go and find Sandy," she said, indicating the door.

"But we haven't finished yet," I said. "There's lots more we need to tell you."

Mrs. Frankish ignored my plea.

There was nothing more we could do. We trooped back to the waiting room and watched the smile drop from Sandy's face as she saw our gloomy expressions.

Rhianna started to cry, and Jamie made a good effort pretending he wasn't about to.

But I just felt numb inside. Too numb to cry.

CHAPTER 47

Rhianna

Sandy put her arms around me and hugged me tight. "What happened?" she asked, looking at Vicky.

Vicky didn't answer. She just shook her head and went and sat down in the corner. She pulled her knees up to her chest and hugged them.

"They told us we had to wait here," I said.

"They don't want us to live with Dad," Jamie said, then he burst into tears.

"I'm so sorry. Really, I am," said Sandy.

"Are they going to send me away to that school now?" I asked her.

"I don't know, Rhianna." Vicky bit her bottom lip.

"They can't make me go, can they? Not if I don't want to?" I looked at Vicky again.

But Vicky didn't say anything. No one said anything. We just sat. And sat. After ages and ages, the door opened and Mrs. Frankish walked in.

CHAPTER 48

Vicky

I tried to search Mrs. Frankish's face for clues to our fate, but she was avoiding our eyes, looking down at the papers she held in her hand.

"My colleagues and I have discussed things in the light of everything you've told us. And we've looked carefully at this prison report on your dad." She looked up. Her expression was serious. I dug my fingertips into my palms and braced myself for the worst. "Apart from absconding, it seems he's been a model prisoner." She paused for a moment. "We've decided to give him a second chance," she said quietly. "We're going to recommend that you return to his care."

Shocked, it took a second for me to take this in.

"But," she continued, "this will only be for a trial period and under very strict supervision. . . ."

Rhianna looked at me for an explanation. Jumping up, I yelled, "We're going to live with Dad!"

There was a huge explosion from Jamie.

"Yessssss!"

Rhi squealed with delight. Jamie was leaping around the room, shouting and cheering and bouncing off the walls. Sandy laughed and hugged Rhi.

"Thank you so much, Mrs. Frankish," I said happily.

She turned to me. "Don't mess up this trial with your dad, Vicky."

"We won't."

She patted my arm with her long bony hand, then, without another word, hurried out of the waiting room.

CHAPTER 49

Rhianna

We had to wait for days and days, but then the letter came. It said we were definitely allowed to live with Dad. Sandy read it and told me. I wanted to go and pack my stuff right away, but Sandy said it was too early because we weren't going for another two weeks, so we had to go to school as usual.

At school I told everyone in my class that we were going to live with Dad. Mrs. Edwards said it was wonderful news and she was really pleased for me. She said I could draw a picture of Dad, Vicky, Jamie and me in our new house, so I drew us standing outside a little white cottage with lovely red roses all around the door. Then I drew a yard with lots of trees and veggies growing in it and six chickens pecking on the ground and two pet rabbits in a big run on the grass. On the other side of our house I drew a big blue lake with a little island in the middle. Last of all, I used Mrs. Edwards's special silver and gold pens to draw Mom and Peter's spirits on the island and stuck sparkly glitter all around them both. I drew one of Mom's arms up in the air because she was waving to us. It took me until break time to finish it. Mrs. Edwards said it was the best picture I'd ever done and pinned it up on the wall.

At break time Maxine and I were walking along the hall when we saw Charlene Slackton. She was standing by the bulletin board with Vomitty Matt. She had her arms around his neck.

As we walked past, she said to me, "What you staring at, Der-Brain?" She looked at me nastily, but I stopped and looked straight back at her.

"I'm not a Der-Brain," I said.

I didn't feel scared of her anymore. Do you know, I just felt cross. She got on my nuckets.

I walked right up to her. I could see lots of pimples underneath her orange makeup.

"I'm not a Der-Brain," I said again.

She took a step back and wobbled a bit on her high heels.

"Only joking . . . ," she said.

Vomitty Matt grinned at me. Charlene turned to him. "What's up with you?" she said.

"Nothing," he said, but he stopped smiling.

When I walked home with Vicky after school, I told her what happened and she laughed.

"It's not funny," I said. "Charlene Slackton's a bully."

"Bet you she won't bully you anymore," Vicky said.

"She better not pick on Maxine either," I said.

Over the weekend, Sandy took us to see Paul and Sarah. We hadn't seen them for weeks. Sarah had come home from the hospital. We went in and Paul was smiling all the time, and he said come and meet our new addition. I didn't understand what he meant, but we followed him upstairs into my old bedroom with the new fluffy duck and rabbit curtains. Sarah was standing next to a wooden crib, and she was smiling too and holding a tiny doll wrapped up in a soft white blanket, except it wasn't a doll. It was a baby. A real live baby.

"Her name's Grace," said Paul, stroking her head with his little finger. "Isn't she beautiful?"

I had a good look, but I wasn't too sure. She didn't look a bit like Baby Emma even before I poked out her eyes. She had lots of tufts of black hair at the sides of her head but was bald on top like a little old man, and she went all red and wrinkly when she cried. But Vicky said she was the most gorgeous baby she had ever seen, so I had another look. Then I put out my finger and Grace grabbed hold of it and wouldn't let it go for ages, but I didn't mind at all because her hand was soft and chubby.

Sarah let me and Vicky take turns holding her. She showed us the right way so we wouldn't drop her and Grace wouldn't feel uncomfortable. Paul and Sarah were still smiling, and I felt good because they were happy, even though there was nowhere to sit down with all the baby stuff and mess everywhere.

Vicky said we were really sorry for running away, and Sarah gave her a hug.

"We're going to live with Dad again," I told them.

"That's fantastic," said Paul. "But we'll miss you all."

"Would you like another doll as a present?" Sarah asked me. I had told her what had happened to Baby Emma at the lake, and she was sorry. She knew I'd had Baby Emma ever since I was little.

"No, thank you," I said. "I'm probably too old for dolls now. Actually, I don't even believe in Santa or that Mrs. Frankish is a witch anymore."

Then I thought for a second. "But I still like little

china penguins that bring you luck. I'm not too grown up for them."

"Maybe we could get you one of those, then?" said Paul with a smile.

"That's okay." I put my hand in my pocket and pulled out the little penguin Elizabeth gave me. "I've already got one. And it's very lucky."

I told them about Elizabeth and her big spooky house and how she saved us from the dogs in the garden. "We're going to go back and see her one day. She lives quite near Daniel."

"So who's Daniel?" asked Sarah.

Vicky went bright red.

"Vicky's boyfriend." I giggled.

"He's not!" said Vicky loudly, but her eyes were all bright and she was grinning.

CHAPTER 50

Vicky

"Vicky?"

At the sound of Daniel's voice, I felt a netful of butterflies flap excitedly inside my stomach.

"How's it going?" he asked.

I could hear Jip barking in the background and wished they were both with me, right here, right now, instead of miles away down the other end of a very long phone line.

"We're going to live with Dad on Saturday," I told him.

"Finally. . . . Bet you can't wait."

"Sandy's been fantastic, but you're right. We're all really excited. And Rhi's had her stuff packed for over a week now."

Daniel laughed.

Then he said something I'd never expected to hear.

"I've . . . I've got some news too. I'm back at school now."

"Really?"

"I started yesterday." He gave another small laugh. "Nearly walked straight out again, but I'm glad I didn't."

"Why, Daniel? Why did you change your mind?" There was a silence. What on earth had happened? I wondered.

"Something to do with this girl I met. . . ."

"Oh." A sudden dart of jealousy stabbed me hard, instantly puncturing all my hopes and dreams.

"Vicky? You still there?"

"Um. Yes . . . of course." I forced myself to sound cheery. "So . . . you . . . you met a girl, then? I mean great, that's great. What's she . . . Is she . . ." I trailed off miserably.

"She's you . . . actually."

Blushing like a beet, I punched the air, dancing in silent celebration. Thank goodness he couldn't see me.

"But . . . I never said you should go back to school."

"No, but you sort of made me think about stuff. Face up to things I didn't want to face up to."

"So, was it okay? What happened?"

"It was all right. As much as double math followed by double French can be on a wet Monday afternoon. It was weird being around so many other people. I suppose I'll get used to it."

"What about the other kids?"

"There's a couple of guys I'm friendly with. We played soccer together at break. They seem okay." He hesitated for a moment. "If . . . if anyone gives me a hard time—and they haven't yet—I think I can handle it now."

I thought back to that last day at the lake when I'd nearly drowned and how he'd kept so calm and in control. I remembered the look on his face when he'd told those bullies to get lost.

"You'll be fine, Dan. I know you will."

"I meant to tell you," he said. "I went back to the cave. I found something on the floor."

"What is it?" I asked.

"It's a surprise. When you've got your new address, let me know and I'll send it to you."

"Okay. Thanks." I wondered if it was one of Rhi's Barbies or even the map we'd bought.

"I really miss you, Vicky," he said suddenly.

The fluttering butterflies in my stomach went loopy, turning backflips in unison. If I were Rosie, I could have instantly replied with something brilliant, witty and wonderful. But I'm me, so my best shot was to tell him the truth.

"I miss you too."

"Come up and stay for school break," he said urgently. "It's not far away. I've already asked my parents. They're cool. They can even lend you our big family tent and camp beds and—you can all come and stay the whole week." He stopped. "I mean . . . that is . . . if . . . if you want to. . . ."

"Daniel, I would love to . . ."

The next day at school, I mentioned Daniel to Rosie.

"Hmmm," she said. "I've had my suspicions you've been concealing a romantic attachment."

She leaned closer.

"So what's he like? You really fancy him, don't you?"

"'Fancy,' Rosie? Fancy? Exactly who have you been hanging around with while I've been away?" I teased.

"Fancy is a perfectly acceptable word—I think you'll find the great William Shakespeare himself uses it in—"

"Come on," I interrupted, taking her arm. "Let's go and sit on the bench. I'll tell you all about Daniel."

We sat down under the big oak tree and watched

the younger kids running around like manic puppies. On the other side of the playground I saw Rhi and Maxine giggling happily together in the sunshine.

"I want to tell you something about my dad too," I said. "It was a big secret once, but it's not anymore."

CHAPTER 51

Rhianna

Vicky says the Prison Housing Adviser has arranged for Dad and us to live in an apartment on the other side of town.

"But I don't want to live in an apartment on the other side of town," I told her. "I want to live near Daniel and the lake in a cottage with a big garden and have chickens and pet rabbits and grow veggies with Dad."

"We can't, Rhi," she said. "Dad said we're really lucky to get this apartment. Besides, if we live there, we won't have to change schools again."

"That's good. But can we live near Daniel one day?"

"Maybe," she said. Then she smiled. "It would be perfect, wouldn't it?"

"Except Jamie would want a smelly goat," I said.

"No way!" She laughed. "They eat your clothes if you stand too near them!"

"What about Daniel?"

"He's invited us up to visit," she said, all excited.

"Really?"

"I asked Dad on the phone last night if we can go."

"What did he say?" I asked.

"Yes . . . if we can afford it. And I'm going to make sure we can afford it. Seeing Paul and Sarah's baby gave me an idea. Now that I'm thirteen, I can earn a bit of money babysitting."

"So we can go back to the island!"

"Yes, but not in that tatty boat, thanks very much. . . ." Vicky grinned at me. "Hey, remember when we went on pedal boats at that theme park years ago? You, me and Mom in one and Dad and Jamie in the other?"

"Yeah, and Dad said let's have a race."

"But we could only make our pedal boat go backward. And Dad was calling out instructions all serious, but then Mom got the giggles, and the more he tried to help, the more she couldn't stop laughing, so we just went around and around in circles till the man called us in . . ."

"And afterward she said it was the best boat ride she'd ever had," I said.

We both laughed. Vicky and me talk about Mom a lot now. Sometimes it makes me feel sad and I cry a bit because I know she's not ever coming home, but other times it makes me feel warm inside to think about her and remember things. I know she's dead and her body doesn't work anymore, but I still think her spirit is on our island. And so does Vicky.

CHAPTER 52

Vicky

It was early Saturday morning, and there was a loud ring on Sandy's doorbell.

"Vicky!" yelled Rhi from downstairs.

I glanced around our bedroom checking that we'd packed everything, picked up our bags and headed out to the landing. Jamie came charging past me and bounded down the stairs three at a time.

"He's here!" he shouted to no one in particular. "Dad's here!"

He flung open the door, and he and Rhi threw themselves into Dad's arms.

"Whoa!" Dad said, laughing as he lifted them off the ground.

"All ready, Vicky?" he asked me.

I nodded, then ran over and hugged him too.

Sandy came up holding a large cake tin.

"Had a spare half hour," she said, handing Rhi the tin. "Brownies."

We all hugged her and thanked her for everything. Then we loaded our stuff into the trunk of the taxi. Sandy promised to come around the following week for dinner. We climbed into the taxi and, as it drove away, waved to Sandy until we turned the corner at the end of her street.

After driving for about fifteen minutes, we pulled up beside a tall apartment building. We unloaded our stuff as Dad paid the driver. I looked up at the concrete tower. Dad glanced at me nervously, but I grinned back at him.

"Relax, Dad. We wouldn't mind living in a cardboard box as long as we could all stay together."

"Are we going to live in a box?" asked Rhi.

"No, we're going to live up there." Dad pointed. "Tenth floor."

Jamie and Rhi tried to count the levels to see which was our floor.

"Come on," I said. "Let's go up."

Inside there was an elevator and stairs. The elevator was noisy, and it made an odd rattling noise, which scared

Rhi a bit, so she clung on to Dad. We got out on the tenth floor and looked around. There were four apartments, each facing a different direction.

"That's ours," said Dad, indicating a door with 42 on it.

The door opposite ours opened. A lady in a sari came out, holding a small child tucked on her hip and a folded stroller in the other hand. She glanced at us warily.

"Hello," said Rhi. "We're coming to live at number forty-two."

"Welcome," she said with a shy smile.

"Thanks," I called as she disappeared into the elevator.

Dad turned the key in our new front door and pushed it open.

"It's in a bit of a state," he said, picking up a brown envelope from the doormat. "But I can fix it up, bit by bit. And there's some furniture arriving soon."

I looked around. Apart from a couple of suitcases and seven large cardboard boxes overflowing with pots and pans, dishes, bedding and other stuff, the apartment was empty. There was a little hallway, a living room, a kitchen, a bathroom and two bedrooms—a small one and an even smaller one. The people who lived here before us had liked bright orange, purple and chocolate brown. A lot. Every room was decorated in a sickly mixture of those colors except for the bathroom, which was totally green—the walls, the floor, the ceiling—even the bathtub, toilet and sink.

"If you and Rhi share the bigger bedroom, Jamie can have the small one, and I'll sleep on the sofa, when it comes," said Dad.

He explained that the prison had fixed up some training for him, restoring furniture at a local project that helped ex-prisoners get back to work, and they were on their way to deliver some pieces so we'd have something to sit on and sleep in. It sounded like the same project Rosie said her dad worked for when I told her all about my dad being in prison.

"But I thought your dad ran some really posh antiques business," I'd told her.

She looked at me and grinned. "Whatever gave you that idea?" she said.

Jamie flung open a door in the sitting room.

"Here's the balcony!" he called.

We followed him out. There was only just room out there for us all.

"No yard, I'm afraid," mumbled Dad.

"I can see a park!" said Jamie, looking out at the fantastic view.

It looked like a much nicer and better-kept park than the one where we used to live. There were two tennis courts, a playground, soccer fields and a boating pond with a little island in the middle.

"We won't need a yard, Dad. We can go there," said Rhi.

I looked down to the street and saw a big van pull up. Two men got out with a girl. To my surprise, she looked up and waved. I did a double take. It was Rosie!

The men started unloading the furniture.

"Let's hope this elevator doesn't break down," murmured Dad as we all hurried down to help.

"Rosie!" I exclaimed when we got outside.

"Thought I'd come and help out." She turned to the tall man. "Dad, this is my friend Vicky."

I looked at him and pasted on a smile. I could feel my face burning bright red. I was sure he was thinking I wasn't the sort of kid Rosie should hang out with.

"Nice to meet you. Come around sometime and pull Rosie's nose out of those books for a bit, will you?"

"Dad! Please!" hissed Rosie, rolling her eyes. "You're soooo embarrassing!"

"That's what dads are for, isn't it?" joked Dad.

Rosie's dad and the other man, Dave, laughed.

"Ha ha. Very funny," I said, grinning at Rosie.

•••

Two hours later, our new apartment had a sofa and two armchairs, bunk beds in Rhi's and my room and a small single bed crammed into Jamie's. We also had a fold-up camping table and four chairs, a wardrobe and two chests of drawers.

After mugs of tea and lots of Sandy's brownies, Rosie, her dad and Dave left us to it, and we set about unpacking the boxes, making up the beds and sorting out our stuff.

Mrs. Frankish swooped in for her first visit later that afternoon. I felt really nervous, and even Jamie was on his best behavior. But I got the feeling she was secretly rooting for us. She gave Dad a cookbook and despite munching her way through three brownies, she insisted on marking all the "nutritionally correct" recipes with her green highlighter. Rhi was definitely not impressed.

"I'm not eating that!" she said, pointing to a photo labeled "Liver and Onion Surprise."

I thought Mrs. Frankish would get all huffy, but she just glanced at the photo, gave a small laugh and told Rhi she didn't blame her.

It was only after Mrs. Frankish had left that I noticed the envelope Dad had picked up from the doormat when we first came in. It was propped on a shelf in Rhi's and my bedroom, tucked behind her little china penguin—Dad must have put it there for safekeeping. It was addressed to me . . . and it was from Daniel.

Inside was the photo Great-Auntie Irene had taken of Dad, Mom, Rhianna, Jamie and me by the lake. So this was what Daniel had found at the cave. I grinned. He'd managed to rescue the one thing that was most precious to us all, and apart from a small tear along one edge, it was undamaged. I gently traced my finger over Mom's smiling face. It's never going to be the same without you, I thought.

But deep inside I had the amazing feeling that a whole new chapter in my life was just beginning. And no matter what happened, as long as Rhi, Dad, Jamie and I were together, everything was going to be all right.